M000283981

DREAMS OF THE WITCH

WITCHES OF KEATING HOLLOW, BOOK 4

DEANNA CHASE

Enjoy!
Deanna Chase

Copyright © 2018 by Deanna Chase

First Edition 2018

Cover Art by Raven

Editing by Angie Ramey

ISBN Print 978-1-940299-72-3

ISBN Ebook 978-1-940299-71-6

All rights reserved. No part of this publication may be reproduced, stored in, or introduced into a retrieval system, or transmitted in any form, or by any means (electronic, mechanical, photocopying, recording, or otherwise) without the prior written permission of both the copyright owner and the publisher of this book.

This book is a work of fiction. Names, characters, places, and incidents are products of the author's imagination or are used fictitiously. Any resemblance to actual events, locals, business establishments, or persons, living or dead, are entirely coincidental.

Bayou Moon Press, LLC

ABOUT THIS BOOK

Welcome to Keating Hollow, the enchanted town full of love, friendship, and family.

Faith Townsend's life is going exactly as planned. The spa she recently opened is thriving and she has a handsome new man in her life. But when she receives a letter from the mother who walked out on her when she was just five years old, Faith's perfect world is turned upside down.

Hunter McCormick has spent the last ten years on the move, trying to outrun his demons. But now that he's found Keating Hollow and Faith Townsend, he's determined to make the town his home. Life is good right up until old secrets are revealed, and Hunter is in danger of losing the only person he's ever cared about. Hunter will have to find a way to re-earn Faith's trust if he wants to be the one to fulfill the dreams of the witch.

CHAPTER 1

"Just one more screw and we'll be in business," Hunter said, his impressive arm muscles flexing as he tightened a bolt on a massage table.

Faith Townsend stared at her contractor and hoped she wasn't drooling. The man was gorgeous with a capital G. Had it really been six months since he'd started working for her, helping her build out her new spa? It seemed like just a few weeks ago that he'd walked in from who-knows-where and started the renovations that had transformed her newly acquired building into the most gorgeous space she'd ever seen.

"Everyone is duly impressed," Faith said. She'd just hosted the soft opening of her brand-new luxury spa that afternoon. Her entire family, along with half the town, had shown up to take a tour and indulge in the fancy spa products her sister Abby had created. The appointment book was already half-filled for the following month, and the feedback had been amazing. "You've outdone yourself, Hunter. My sister Noel is interested in having you do some work on her inn when you have an opening in your schedule, and my other sister Yvette said she might have work for you, too."

He gave the bolt one last tug and straightened, turning to look at her. A slow smile spread across his ruggedly handsome face. "Are you trying to get rid of me, Faith? I thought you still needed your office painted."

She definitely *wasn't* trying to get rid of him. If anything, she'd been racking her brain for the past two weeks, trying to drum up more work so she would have an excuse to see him every day. "Nope. They were just so impressed they were trying to steal you away. I told them they'd have to wait, though. I've decided to go ahead with the outdoor relaxation retreat area we talked about last month. You did say you could build a stone fire pit, right?"

He laughed. "Sure. Anything you want." He stuffed the socket wrench in his back pocket. "Did you want the waterfall and rock wall we talked about, too?"

"Yes, please." Faith grinned at him, wondering how long it would take for him to transform the outside. It was still summer in Keating Hollow, and if he could get it done within the next few months, her clients could still enjoy the outdoors before the dreary, rainy season rolled in. "If you're not too busy, that is."

He winked. "I'm all yours until further notice."

Faith's breath caught, and her heart skipped a beat. She'd developed a crush on this guy the day he'd started working for her. The fact that he'd shown up early, seemed to thoroughly enjoy his work, and stayed ahead of schedule had won her over. It certainly didn't hurt that he was gorgeous and thoughtful. He never failed to bring her a mocha from Incantation Café every morning, and when he went out for

2

lunch, he always remembered to ask if she wanted anything. They'd formed a comfortable relationship, and she was going to miss him when his work at the spa was done.

"Hunter?" she asked, her voice slightly shaky.

"Yeah?" He glanced up from the clipboard in his hands.

"Can I take you to dinner tonight?" she asked, hearing the nervous tremble in her voice. "As a thank you for all the work you've done? This place wouldn't be anywhere near ready to open if not for you."

"Dinner?" He frowned. "You don't have to do that. I was just doing my job."

She let out a small huff of laughter. "And taking care of me every day, making sure I eat and take a day off here and there. You even made me go to the healer a few weeks ago when that cough wouldn't go away." Faith walked up to him and put a light hand on his arm. "You've been more than just my contractor. You have to know that. We're... friends. Right?"

His dark eyes searched hers, the intensity making her heat from the inside out. The expression on his face was anything but friendly. There was pure desire reflecting back at her, and suddenly she had an image of him tossing her onto the massage table and the two of them going at it like teenagers. Her entire body tingled with anticipation.

"Faith?" Footsteps sounded on the wood floors just outside the half-open door. "Are you back here?"

Hunter took a step back and gave his head a shake as if to clear his thoughts.

Damn. Faith was going to kill Yvette. Her timing was the absolute worst.

"We need to get going," Yvette called, clearly still looking for Faith.

"In here," Faith called, giving Hunter a defeated smile.

"There you are," Yvette said as she pushed the door open. Her oldest sister had her dark hair piled onto the top of her head, curls framing her radiant face. She glowed with happiness, and Faith instantly forgave her for interrupting the moment. She'd just gotten engaged a few hours ago when her boyfriend Jacob had popped the question. Yvette was getting everything she wanted and deserved, including being stepmom to the sweetest little girl on the planet. "Jacob and I need to get going. Skye is ready to pass out."

"Of course." Faith turned to Hunter. "Don't go anywhere. We still need to discuss dinner."

He shrugged. "I'm not in a hurry."

"Good." She hooked her arm through Yvette's. "I'll walk you out."

The sisters exited the massage room and were silent until they rounded the corner at the end of the hall.

"Oh. Em. Gee," Yvette said in a loud whisper. "What did I just walk in on?"

Faith blinked. "What do you mean?"

"Come on, little sister. There was so much sexual tension in that room that I'm surprised no one burst into flames. And you mentioned something about dinner."

"I want to take him to dinner to thank him for all his hard work." Faith paused and blew out a breath. "It was pretty heated, wasn't it?" she said, fanning herself. They were standing in the relaxation room where eventually her female clients would relax while waiting for their appointments. Comfortable lounge chairs were arranged around the room, and an elaborate refreshment bar was tucked into one corner. Faith walked over and filled a cup with cucumber water. After downing the liquid, she refilled the cup and turned to look at her sister. "I think he was getting ready to kiss me. But then..."

"I interrupted you," Yvette finished with a wince. "I'm sorry, Faith. I wouldn't have barged in if I'd known."

"Of course you wouldn't have." Faith waved a hand and threw her cup into the garbage. "Don't give it another thought. If it's meant to be, there'll be another chance soon enough." She gave her sister a wicked grin, grabbed her hand, and tugged her back into the hall and through the door that led to the reception area.

"Ready?" Jacob asked as he lifted his daughter into his arms.

"I'll be right behind you." Yvette kissed Skye on the cheek and tenderly caressed the baby's head. Jacob's expression melted as he watched the two people he loved most in the world.

Faith's heart lurched against her ribcage as she watched the tender moment. It was enough to turn even the most jaded person into a pile of goo. The glow radiating from Yvette practically blinded Faith, and she couldn't help but wonder if she'd ever find someone who lit her up in the same way.

Jacob smiled at Faith. "Congratulations. The place looks fantastic. No doubt you're going to have a line out the door in no time."

"From your lips to the goddess's ears," Faith said, pointing upward.

As Jacob took Skye outside, Yvette stepped in close to her sister and wrapped her arms around her. "The place really is wonderful."

"Thanks." Faith hugged her sister Yvette tightly, blinked back tears, and whispered, "Congratulations. You deserve this so much. Jacob and Skye are lucky to have you."

Yvette squeezed Faith and said, "I'm the lucky one. Jacob and Skye managed to steal my heart, and it's hard for me to even remember what my life was like before Jacob walked into it."

Good, Faith thought. Six months ago, Yvette had been newly divorced and stuck with a new business partner she hadn't wanted. But lucky for her, the new business partner had turned out to be Jacob, and after a few bumps in the road, they'd fallen hard for each other. Faith was overjoyed for her, but she couldn't help the empty ache that seemed permanently lodged in her chest.

All of her sisters were blissfully happy with their blended families, and what did she have? Not much besides her family, a demon puppy, and a new business with plenty of debt and negative cash flow. If she was lucky, it would be a good six months to a year before she could expect to see her monthly numbers turning from red to black. The realization was daunting to say the least. She'd bet everything on her new business. Failing wasn't an option.

After her sister and the rest of her guests left, she glanced around at her gorgeous new high-end spa, A Touch of Magic, and knew there was only one thing missing—someone to share it with.

As if on cue, Hunter appeared from the back and flashed his sexy half-smile at her. "About that dinner offer… What time should I pick you up?"

A slow smile spread across Faith's face as everything inside of her turned to mush. This was what she wanted, someone to share and celebrate her accomplishments. "Seven-thirty? Cozy Cave? I hear they have a trout special that will make your mouth water."

His gaze dropped to her lips, and before she knew it, he was standing right in front of her, one arm snaked around her waist. "There's only one thing that's been making my mouth water, and it sure as hell isn't a piece of fish."

She opened her mouth to respond, but before she could get any words out, his mouth covered hers and he kissed her so thoroughly her head began to spin. Faith forgot everything else except the tall, muscular man whose kiss was making her toes curl. She wanted to lose herself in him, wrap herself around him, and explore every inch of his rock-hard frame.

"Seven-thirty," he said as he pulled away.

"Huh?" She was dazed and didn't understand why his lips had left hers.

"Dinner. I'll pick you up at your place." He pressed one more soft kiss on her lips, and then he was gone.

Faith pressed her hand to her tingling lips, trying to keep the sensation from fading. Had that really happened? She glanced in the mirror behind the front desk and took in her flushed cheeks and the slight glow of happiness in her bright blue eyes.

Yes. Hunter had kissed her, and he was picking her up in two hours for dinner.

With a new lightness in her heart, Faith closed up the spa and hurried home to her small blue cottage on the edge of town. It was a two-bedroom fixer-upper her dad had helped her purchase at auction a few years back. Once her spa started to make money, she'd be paying him back with interest. After playing with and feeding Xena, her shih tzu devil dog, she showered then spent forty-five minutes trying on everything in her wardrobe until she settled on a pair of skinny jeans and a silky halter top that showed off her tanned shoulders. After taking care to do her makeup, she studied herself and nodded. The witch staring back at her was casual but sexy. Perfect.

With five minutes to spare, Faith sat on her couch, Xena in her lap, and waited. And waited. And waited some more. When two hours had passed, she was contemplating calling the town healer or Drew, the town deputy sheriff, just to put her mind at ease that nothing had happened to him. But finally, her phone chimed with a text alert.

It was from Hunter. *Sorry, Faith. Something's come up, and I had to cut out of town. I'll have to take a raincheck.*

She glanced at the clock, incredulous. He couldn't have texted earlier? Fuming, she broke out a bottle of wine, silently cursing the opposite sex. Her plans with Hunter had been the first date she'd had in over a year, and she'd just been stood up.

CHAPTER 2

"*F*aith, hurry. It's freezing out here," Abby called from her golf cart. All three of Faith's sisters were bundled up in scarves, gloves, and thick jackets. It was the Sunday evening after Thanksgiving, and the temperature in Keating Hollow was dropping quickly. The day had been in the sixties, but since the sun had gone down, the wind had picked up, and if the temperature stayed above freezing they'd be lucky.

"Keep your pants on. I'm coming," Faith called as she grabbed an envelope that was just lying in the middle of her lawn. She must've dropped it after she'd emptied her mailbox the day before.

They were headed to Yvette's bookstore where they were planning a holiday-themed bridal shower for Noel, who'd finally set a date with her fiancé, Drew. They'd decided to tie the knot on Christmas Eve at the Townsend family home. Faith held the letter up, squinting at it in the moonlight. Her name and address were inscribed in unfamiliar handwriting, and there was no return address. She bit down on her bottom lip, trying to speculate who it might be from. No one came to mind.

"Hanna's waiting for us," Abby said from the driver's seat of the golf cart. Her long blond hair was pulled back in a braid that poked out from under her knitted cap.

"Relax. She's not going to start without us, is she?" Faith asked as she climbed into the back seat next to Noel, stuffing the envelope in her pocket. She'd take a look at it later.

"She's bringing cookies," Noel said. "And you know she can't control herself once she digs in."

Faith snorted. Hanna worked at Incantation Café where she was surrounded by cookies all day, every day. But Noel was right. Hanna refrained from indulging while she was working, but once she clocked out? All bets were off. The wind picked up, and Faith shivered slightly. "Why are we tooling around in the open-air-mobile?"

"Have you forgotten about the golf cart races later?" Abby asked. "Wanda is meeting us with Irish coffees for everyone after we finish planning the shower."

"Right." Faith huddled in close to Noel, noting she had changed her hair again. In the last year, she'd gone from bright red, to blond, to strawberry blond. Now it was auburn with bright red streaks. "Nice do. Love the bangs."

Noel grinned. "Thanks. Drew said he felt a little naughty, like he'd been given permission to fool around with the town's new hottie. He says that every time I change my hair."

Faith laughed, but inside she felt a twinge of jealousy. Not because she had a thing for her sister's fiancé, but because even though she'd finally been on a few dates in the last couple months, there wasn't anyone in sight who had long-term potential. And there certainly wasn't anyone she thought was actual boyfriend material, much less someone she might actually consider marrying. "At least you know what to do if things ever get stale in the bedroom."

Noel gave Faith a secretive smile. "That's not something I'm too terribly worried about."

"Stop! No one wants to hear about your bedroom antics," Yvette called over her shoulder. Of the four Townsend girls, she was the only one with naturally dark hair. It was a beautiful chestnut color, and Faith often wished she'd been blessed with Yvette's gorgeous locks. Her own hair was light blond and boring, in her opinion. Maybe she'd go to Noel's colorist and try something new for a change.

Abby snickered. "I bet Faith wouldn't mind some details. How long has it been, little sister?"

"Since what?" Faith asked absently, still wondering if she had the guts to dye her hair.

"Since you had a hot guy in your bed," Noel explained as Abby cackled.

Faith rolled her eyes. "Way too long."

"Hey," Noel said, nudging her. "Didn't you go out with Jacob's friend Brian last week? How'd that go?"

Abby pulled the cart into a spot in front of Yvette's bookstore, and Faith's attention locked on the enchanted front window where Santa and his reindeer were flying over a village that was being covered with a light snowfall. Ice skaters were twirling on the rink in the center while a witch and her familiar stood off to the side, wand in hand. A stack of books titled *A Witchin' Christmas* was prominently displayed off to the left.

"The window is gorgeous, Vette. Did you and Jacob do that today?" she asked as she turned back around to find all three of her sisters staring at her. "What?"

Yvette tsked. "No one cares about the window at the moment. We want to hear about your date."

Faith shrugged. "We just had coffee and took a walk down by the river. Nothing special."

"That's it?" Yvette asked. "Did you like him? Are you going out again?"

Brian was Yvette's fiancé's best friend, and he'd moved to Keating Hollow earlier in the year. Yvette had set Faith up with him and was a little too invested in the outcome. The date had been fine. He was funny and interesting to talk to, but there hadn't been any spark. At least not on her end. It was too bad, too, because there was no denying Brian was gorgeous and a good guy. Faith frowned. "He said he'd call and maybe we'd get dinner."

"Let me guess... he hasn't called yet," Yvette said. Without waiting for an answer, she continued. "Well, it was just Thanksgiving, and I think he headed down to southern California to see his family. I'm sure he'll get in touch when he gets back in town."

"Sure." Faith hopped out of the golf cart. "Let's get inside. It's cold out here." Holding the door to Keating Hollow Books open, Faith waved her sisters in. She followed Noel, who paused just inside the door, glancing around at the evening customers still milling around the place. The shop was closing in twenty minutes, and there was quite a line at the checkout counter. Yvette's Black Friday weekend sale seemed to have been a huge hit.

"Your date didn't exactly sweep you off your feet, did he?" Noel asked, pulling Faith over into the corner.

Faith let out a frustrated sigh. "No, dammit. And the worst part is, I'm not even sure why not. He's the whole package, and yet... I don't know. We just didn't seem to have any chemistry."

Noel gave her a sympathetic smile and linked an arm through her sister's. "Maybe you just need to give it more time. Get to know him a little before you write him off. You never know. Once you get your hands on him, that might change. If not, there's no harm in making a new friend."

"Friendship. Right," Faith said with a laugh. "I'm sure that's exactly what he's looking for."

"Faith?" a familiar male voice called.

Her blood pressure spiked as she glanced up and spotted Hunter, her former contractor and the man who'd stood her up five months ago when he'd left town for some sort of emergency. He'd never returned, and she'd never heard from him again. He was slightly thinner than when she'd last seen him, and his brown hair was a tad darker, but his sexy five-o'clock shadow woke the butterflies in her stomach. Now that was chemistry.

"Hunter?" she sputtered. "What are you...?" Her voice trailed off as her gaze landed on the pretty raven-haired woman standing beside him, a stack of children's books in her hands.

"Sorry," he said quickly, a tinge of nervousness in his voice. "This is Vivian. She's an old friend."

"Right." Faith forced herself to hold her hand out to the woman. "I'm Faith Townsend. I own A Touch of Magic, the town's new spa. You should come by, get a massage or a facial. Hunter knows where it's at."

"A massage sounds lovely," she said, shaking Faith's hand. "I can't remember the last time I treated myself."

"Faith is the best therapist around," Hunter said.

He should know, Faith thought. She'd given him more free massages than she could count during the time he'd worked for her. The man had done some fabulous work; he'd deserved it. She could still feel his hard, well-defined muscles beneath her fingertips. A shiver of desire ran down her spine as she recalled how beautiful he was beneath his clothes. Too bad he'd cut and run right after he kissed her for the first time and then apparently wasted no time finding himself a replacement.

Noel stepped up and introduced herself to Vivian and then smiled at Hunter. "It's good to see you again."

They made their pleasantries, and Noel excused herself. As she made her way over to the café where Abby and Yvette were waiting with Hanna, she glanced over her shoulder and widened her eyes at Faith. *Whoa*, she mouthed. *What is he doing here?*

Faith gave her sister a tiny shake of her head. She had no idea, but as far as she was concerned, he could just turn around and go back to wherever he'd come from. The effect his presence had on her was way too intense, despite the fact that he was clearly taken. Out of bounds. Off limits. Throwing herself at him would be very bad form.

"I should—" she started.

"I was going to call you tomorrow," Hunter said, cutting her off as he shoved his hands into the pockets of his jeans.

"Tomorrow?" she asked, with a huff of humorless laughter. "Better late than never, I guess."

He winced. "I deserve that."

Vivian glanced between the two of them then started to back up. "I think that's my cue. Hunter, I'll just go pay for these and wait for you outside."

"Thanks," he said without taking his eyes off Faith.

"She's lovely," Faith said. "Congratulations."

He frowned. "What?"

"Vivian. She's really pretty." Faith glanced away, wondering what the hell she was doing. Why was she standing there behaving so awkwardly? It wasn't as if she'd actually dated Hunter. They'd had one hot kiss. That was it. Sure, she'd seen him fully naked, but that had been an accident and what had arguably escalated her desire to get her hands all over him outside of the massage table. But she had no claim on him and absolutely no right to be acting like a jealous ex.

"Vivian is my best friend's wife," he said, his tone strange, almost as if it pained him to speak the words.

Her attention snapped back to him. "She's already married?"

He sighed and ran a hand through his hair, exhaustion lining his beautiful features. "She was. Craig was in a bad car accident the day I left Keating Hollow and was in the hospital for almost a month before he lost his battle. That's why I had to leave so suddenly, Faith. I've been in Las Vegas helping Viv with the aftermath of Craig's death ever since."

Shock rendered Faith speechless. Of all the things she'd imagined he'd say if he ever came back, the death of his best friend wasn't one of them. She blinked up at him, suddenly ashamed of all the bad thoughts she'd had concerning him over the past few months. He'd been grieving a profound loss, and she'd been mentally cursing him for leaving without a word. In her defense, they had at the very least been friends, and it had hurt that he'd disappeared from her life with no explanation.

Taking a step closer, she reached out and grabbed his hand. As she squeezed, she said, "I'm so sorry, Hunter. I can't even imagine how hard that would be." Faith quickly glanced at Hanna, her best friend, and felt her heart lurch. If Faith were to suddenly lose her, she had no idea how she'd handle it. Probably no better than Abby had handled Charlotte's loss a decade ago.

"Thank you. I still should've called. Things were just... I'm sorry." He visibly swallowed, appearing to choke down emotion. "There was a lot going on."

"Of course. You don't need to apologize, and you don't need to explain further." She dropped his hand and stepped back. "Are you in town for a while, or are you just passing through?"

Vivian reappeared before he could answer, a canvas bag with the *Keating Hollow Books* logo clutched in her hand. "I'm sorry to interrupt, but Zoey is hungry. We need to get some real food into her soon, or we'll be entering meltdown mode."

It was then that Faith noticed a young girl of about six or seven hiding behind Vivian's legs. She was holding a stuffed dog and reaching for Hunter's hand. She wrapped her fingers around one of his, and he smiled down at her.

"Ready for dinner, little Z?" he asked.

She nodded and stared at Faith with wide dark eyes.

"Okay. We're going." He shifted his attention back to Faith. "Before we go, I was wondering if you needed any more work done at the spa. If you haven't gotten around to the outdoor area, I could come by in the morning—"

Faith held her hand up, stopping him as she tried to swallow her sudden irritation. For a minute there, she'd been starting to think he'd missed her. That he really had felt bad for leaving her hanging. And while she certainly understood the heartbreaking circumstances, she didn't like feeling as if she were only important because she might be able to provide a paycheck. "Sorry, Hunter. We don't have any construction projects in the works right now."

"I see." He stared down at her, his eyes clouding with something she couldn't read.

Was that disappointment? She couldn't tell, but it was enough that it had her touching his arm gently. "But if you need work, check with my dad. I know he has some stuff around the farm he's been looking to get done. Rebuilding the barn and some fencing. Nothing high end, but it pays."

"Right. Thanks, I'll drop in on him tomorrow." He nodded to Vivian. "We better get our little one fed before it gets too late."

"It was nice to meet you, Faith," Vivian said.

"You too," Faith called as the three of them walked out the door. His voice echoed in her mind, repeating *our little one*. *Ours.* It was as if he'd stepped right into his best friend's shoes and ended up with an instant family.

Was there something going on between them? It wouldn't be the first time two people had turned to each other in grief. If they weren't together, what was Vivian doing in Keating Hollow?

Our. That word still hung there, haunting her. Of course they were together. And if they weren't, they would be soon. They'd just spent the last five months together, leaning on each other during the worst possible scenario. If they weren't finding comfort in each other, she'd be shocked.

"Holy hell," Abby said, appearing right next to Faith. "That looked brutal."

She side-eyed her sister. "You have no idea."

"Come on, baby sis. Hanna spiked the apple cider, and it looks like you could use a cup."

"Make it a double," Faith said, letting Abby tug her through the store.

CHAPTER 3

*H*unter sat on the edge of Zoey's bed, tucking her in. Her dark curly hair was splayed across the pillow, and her favorite stuffed dog was tucked in next to her. He turned the page of her newest book and said, "The end."

She gave him a tired smile. "Again."

He chuckled and would've indulged her if she hadn't already nodded off in the middle of the story the first time. "Not tonight, pumpkin." He leaned down and pressed a light kiss to her forehead. "Time to rest up. Tomorrow's a big day. Mommy's going to take you to your new school."

She frowned but snuggled in closer to him and hugged her dog tighter.

"G'night, little Z," he said, brushing her curls out of her eyes. "See you in the morning."

"Night, Uncle Hunter," she said sleepily, her eyes already closed.

Uncle Hunter. The words stabbed him right in the heart, and he had to choke down his emotion. Because of the distance between Hunter and Craig's family, it had only been in the past five months that Hunter had been able to spend any significant amount of time with the sweet little girl cuddled up next to him. Unsurprisingly, it hadn't taken any time at all for her to wrap him around her little pinky finger and give his life a new purpose. There wasn't anything he wouldn't do for her, even if it meant living with Vivian.

"Is she asleep?" Vivian asked when he walked into the small kitchen. She was sitting at the table, her sock-clad feet propped on one of the chairs.

He nodded, pulled a beer out of the fridge, and popped the top. After taking a long pull, he joined her at the table. Exhaustion swept over him. He'd been up since three in the morning, driving them the last leg of the trip from Las Vegas to Keating Hollow. He'd wanted to get to town before dark so they could set up Zoey and Vivian's bed in his spare bedroom. They'd be sharing for the time being until they worked out better arrangements.

After unloading the U-Haul and setting up their room, the trio had headed into town for dinner and groceries. They'd only ended up in the bookstore after Zoey's eyes lit up when she spotted the window display. She loved reading with her mom at night, and Hunter hadn't been able to resist bringing her a little happiness.

If he'd known he was going to run into Faith, he might have skipped the trip inside. He'd been anxious to see her, but he hadn't wanted to spring Vivian and Zoey on her right away. During the time he'd worked for her, it had been torture to stay away. Damn, he'd wanted her. Wanted her bad. But he'd been working for her, and it wasn't his style to mix business with pleasure. That was the only reason he'd kept his distance. Otherwise, he'd have had her in his bed months before. He was sure of it. There'd been no denying the sparks that had erupted every time they came within three feet of each other, and nothing had changed. He'd felt the same pull the moment he'd laid eyes on her at the bookstore. But now things were... complicated.

"What are your plans for tomorrow?" Vivian asked him. "Are you going to come with us to get Zoey registered in school?"

"If you want." He leaned back in the chair, staring her in the eye. "But after that I need to catch up with a few business contacts and see about finding new work."

"I could go with you," she said with a small smile. "Charm your clients. I'm good at that."

He shook his head and bit back a harsh reply. She'd been hinting about managing his business ever since they'd decided she and Zoey would move to Keating Hollow. But he was still getting used to sharing his home life with her. Sharing his business definitely wasn't in the cards. "I don't think that's the best idea. I've got it covered. But you can look around town and see if anyone's hiring."

She let out a bark of humorless laughter. "I doubt any of these dinky little businesses are looking for a sales rep. Keating Hollow isn't exactly a metropolis bustling with commerce."

Vivian had worked for an organic skin care company and had been on track for a promotion before Craig had been hospitalized. After his accident she'd made the choice to leave to be by his side and to care for Zoey. Hunter narrowed his eyes at her, not liking the judgment in her tone. "Just give it a chance, Vivian. Keating Hollow is full of successful people. They just might surprise you."

She stared at him, her eyes widening in surprise. No doubt she'd recognized the irritation in his tone. She brushed her dark hair behind one ear, and her cheeks flushed as she glanced down. "Sorry. I didn't mean for that to come out sounding so judgmental. I'm just unsettled."

He immediately felt like a jerk. Of course she was. She'd just lost her husband of seven years and uprooted her entire life to a new town where she knew no one but him. He sucked in a breath and tried to be helpful. "Check with Abby Townsend. She has a successful line of magic-infused soaps and lotions. If she's looking to expand, she might be interested. Or try Miss Maple at A Spoon Full of Sugar. Her chocolates are hands down the best on the west coast."

"Okay, sure." She didn't sound convinced, but Hunter knew once she saw for herself how impressive their businesses were, she'd be salivating to get her hands on their products.

He sucked down the rest of his beer and stood. "It's late. I'm headed to bed. Do you need anything?"

"Yes," she said, getting to her feet and walking down the hall toward his bedroom.

He hurried to catch up with her. "Towels are in the bathroom closet along with extra toiletries. There are extra blankets in the hall closet. And if you need to adjust the temperature, the thermostat is at the other end of the hall. If you need more pillows—"

"Hunter," she said, cutting him off as she turned and pressed a light hand to his chest. "I already know all of that. That's not..." She shook her head. "Maybe we should finish this conversation in your bedroom."

He frowned as he stared down at her. "Why?"

Her lips curved into a small, secretive smile, and she ran her hand over his shoulder and down his arm until she clasped his hand in hers and squeezed lightly. "Well, I was thinking it's probably time to take our relationship to the next level."

Hunter took a step back, breaking the connection. "I don't think that's a good idea."

"Sure it is. Zoey is crashed out. Nothing short of a fire alarm would wake her up now. And don't tell me you haven't thought about it. We were good together once, and there's no reason why we can't be good together again. We always did have a good time in the bedroom."

"This can't happen. You were married to my best friend," he said, trying to ease the blow of his rejection. They'd dated a long time ago, before she'd hooked up with Craig. He hadn't been in love with her then, and he wasn't in love with her now. What she was suggesting was never going to happen. Because of Craig and Zoey, he'd be there for her always, but being her lover was off the table.

She glanced down briefly, and when she looked back up at him, her eyes were slightly glassy. "He's gone, Hunter. He wouldn't want me to stop living. You know that as well as I do. Is it really so awful to want to find comfort in someone's arms? He loved you, too. He'd understand."

Hunter's blood ran cold. "Viv, stop. I've already stolen too much from him as it is. This isn't going to happen. Let it go, please."

She sighed. "You're just saying that because you feel guilty."

"No, I don't. Go to bed, Vivian. I'll see you in the morning." Hunter turned and quietly let himself into his bedroom, closing the door behind him.

CHAPTER 4

"So we're set. The shower will be at Yvette's store two weeks from tomorrow, and the bachelorette party will be a week after that in San Francisco," Abby said. "Did we miss anything?"

"Who's responsible for the booze?" Faith asked. She was sitting at one of the small café tables with Hanna, nervously picking at yet another cookie. Ever since Hunter had left, she'd been unable to relax and was currently nibbling on her sixth confection.

Abby chuckled. "Don't worry, I'm on it. Wine has already been ordered."

"Better include some vodka," Hanna whispered. "Now that Hunter is back in the picture, I don't think wine is gonna cut it."

Faith gave her friend an appreciative grin. "You know me so well."

Hanna raised a cookie that was decorated just like the bookstore and nudged it against Faith's in a show of solidarity. "Wine makes everything better. Vodka makes you not care."

"Did someone say wine?" Wanda called as she swept inside the store holding two bottles. Her bright red hair was electric under the florescent lights, and her face glowed with mischief. "Wanda to the rescue."

"Me!" Faith raised her empty cider cup. "Fill me up."

Wanda wound through the café, filling cups, and finally took a seat next to Abby. "I have a surprise for everyone."

"Something better than wine?" Faith took a long sip of the cabernet, trying to drink just enough to numb the complicated feelings she'd been having ever since her run-in with Hunter.

"Nothing's better than wine." She laughed. "But this is good, too." She waved a hand toward the front window.

The door slammed open again, and this time, Clay stumbled in, followed by Drew, Brian, and Rhys. They each had a beer in their hands, and their apparent ringleader, Abby's husband Clay, raised both arms out to the side, gave everyone a lopsided grin, and said, "Let the races begin!"

Faith's gaze met Brian's. He smiled at her, his gorgeous eyes twinkling with interest. The interaction did wonders for her ego, and she wondered if her sister was right when she suggested she'd written him off too soon.

Abby let out a squeal and jumped up out of her chair. "Did you steal Dad's golf cart?"

Clay draped an arm over her shoulders. "More like borrowed. We couldn't let you ladies have all the fun, now could we?"

"Excellent. You're going down, Garrison."

"You wish," he said good naturedly before giving her a lingering kiss on the lips.

When he pulled away, Abby asked, "Where's Olive? With you mother?"

"Yes. She has Daisy, too," he said, giving her another kiss on the nose.

"Where's Jacob?" Yvette asked, inquiring after her fiancé.

Brian, Jacob's best friend, said, "He's watching Skye. Said to have fun and he'll see you when you get home."

A gentle smile claimed Yvette's lips. "He sure does love that little girl."

"Don't we all," Brian agreed.

Abby pulled away from Clay, waved at Rhys, his assistant at the brewery, and then turned to her husband, her eyes narrowed in challenge. "Okay, now that you're here for the golf cart races, what are the stakes?"

He blinked. "Stakes? Aren't bragging rights enough?"

"No way!" Wanda exclaimed. "That's a given. We need something more. A wager that has some teeth. Something epic like when we were in high school. Remember the look on Mr. Johnson's face when he walked out of his front door and found Santa and Mrs. Claus dressed in leathers and all of his reindeer in compromising positions?"

Laughter burst from the group, and Faith's mouth dropped open. "That was you guys?" She was the youngest of the group and hadn't been privy to their shenanigans back then. "I need details."

Drew and Clay shared an amused look then both pointed at Abby and Wanda. "Those two are the culprits," Clay said. "They made a bet that we couldn't get Miss Maple's secret recipe for her caramel-bourbon balls. But Drew here charmed it out of her with his youthful good looks and sparkling personality."

"Please," Noel said. "He got it in a trade because she wanted the secret ingredient in his grandmother's famous chocolate fantasy tart."

"It worked, didn't it?" Drew said, puffing his chest out. "And Abby, Wanda, and Charlotte, ended up turning Mr. Johnson's winter wonderland into a kinkster's holiday fantasy." Laughter burst from his lips, and he practically doubled over from the hilarity of it all. "Can you even imagine Charlotte positioning Rudolph with his nose in Vixen's hindquarters?"

Everyone joined in on the laughter as they imagined Charlotte, the sweetest, kindest one of them all, blushing as she arranged the reindeer into compromising positions. Faith glanced at Hanna, Charlotte's younger sister. She had a bittersweet smile as she indulged in the memory of her late sister. They'd lost Charlotte on the night of her senior prom to an autoimmune disease not even the witches of Keating Hollow could fight.

Faith leaned closer to her. "You okay?"

Hanna nodded and wiped at her eyes. Though the tears appeared to be happy ones. "It's good to talk about her. We don't do that enough."

Faith squeezed her friend's hand and nodded. "I agree."

Abby clasped her hands together in excitement. "I've got it! The losers of the golf cart race have to dress up like Santa's little helpers and perform "Santa Baby" for the town at the holiday carnival. But the winners get to choose the outfits."

Rhys raised one eyebrow. "You want us to sing?"

"No, man," Clay said. "They'll be the ones singing. With the four of us working together we can't lose."

"Anything goes?" Drew asked. "This isn't a magic-free zone, right?"

"Definitely not a magic free zone," Wanda said. "Who's ready?"

Abby and Noel jumped up, grabbing their men along the way. Ever since Abby had gotten her tricked-out golf cart, she and Wanda had formed a friendly rivalry, engaging in races at least once a month. They were constantly coming up with spells that would help their carts and slow down the others.

Faith shook her head. The men were in trouble here. They had no idea what they were getting into.

Brian walked over to her and held his hand out. "Are you ready for this?"

Faith smiled up at him, warmed by his attention. "Sure. Are you?"

He shook his head. "No. But I'm riding in your cart, so I'm feeling confident I won't be on the losing team."

She chuckled. "Smooth."

"Thanks."

"I thought this was a battle-of-the-sexes type thing," she said. "You don't think they're going to disown you if you defect to the estrogen zone?"

He shrugged. "If they were smart they'd follow my lead."

Faith grinned at him. He really was being awfully cute. "Okay then. Let's follow Wanda. We have a better chance with her."

He swept his hand out in front of him and gave a sweeping bow. "Lead on."

Chuckling, Faith grabbed Hanna's arm and the two of them hurried out to Wanda's cart with Brian on their heels.

"Faith!" Yvette called once she was situated in Abby's cart, the flashing purple lights overhead casting an eerie glow. "What are you doing?"

"Riding with Wanda," she called as Wanda whipped the cart out of the parking space and headed down Main Street. "Try to keep up!"

Hanna, who was in the front, shared a glance with Wanda, and they both cracked up.

"Your sisters are never gonna let you live this down," Wanda said.

Faith shrugged. "They'll get over it."

"Rebel, huh?" Brian asked, grinning at her. "I like a girl who's not afraid to take chances."

"I bet," Faith said, shaking her head. "Are you ready for this, Brian? You know these races are brutal, right?"

He raised one eyebrow. "I heard they get a little intense. How far can I expect this to go? We're not talking about maiming anyone, are we?"

"No maiming," Faith said. "But Yvette let a fireball get away from her last time and singed off one of Wanda's eyebrows. She now has next-level skill with the eyebrow pencil."

"I still can't believe she did that," Wanda said, shaking her head. "Of course, I returned the favor by burning the outline of a giant penis in her front yard. Before she noticed it, a neighbor saw it and gave her hell for her rampant depravity." She laughed so hard she wheezed. "Gods, I wish I'd have been there for that."

Brian's eyes widened in mock horror. "You people scare me."

"You love us," Hanna said, batting her eyelashes at him.

He grinned at her, leaned back, and draped an arm across the back of the seat he shared with Faith. And when his hand landed on her shoulder, she didn't shrink away. In fact, his touch was kind of nice.

Wanda turned the cart onto the special golf cart path that ran through the town. The magical river was to the right with mystical redwood trees behind it. She came to a stop and jumped out. After rummaging through a small locker strapped to the back of the cart, she produced four mugs and a thermos full of Irish Coffee. "Who needs something to warm them up?"

Everyone raised a hand.

"Okay, we need a plan," Wanda said. "All magic on deck, so to speak. I'm fire, Faith and Hanna are water. Brian, what about you?"

"Fire," he said, smiling down at Faith, one of his dimples charming her. "Opposites attract, right?"

"Sure," she laughed nervously, both amused and slightly anxious about his flirting. Did he have to turn it on so thick in front of her friends?

"Hmm, would've been better if we had an earth or air witch in this party." Wanda eyed the other two golf carts as they turned onto the path. "We won't be able to beat them with magic, since they'll have more elements covered, but we might be able to distract them." She kneeled down and whispered something to Brian, leaving Faith and Hanna to wonder what they might be planning.

"Hey!" Hanna said. "You can't leave us out of this. What's the secret?"

But before Wanda could spill the beans, Abby came to a stop right beside them and called, "Ready to get your asses kicked?"

Wanda gave her a wicked grin. "Please. I've toasted you the last six times we've raced. But good luck to you."

Clay leaned over and said something to Drew, and the two let out loud guffaws of laughter.

"They're up to something," Abby said to Wanda as she eyed them suspiciously.

Wanda shrugged as she climbed back into the driver's seat. "No rules, remember?"

"Right. No rules," Clay echoed, still chortling.

"Oh, man. I think we're in for some serious shenanigans," Abby told Yvette. "Better get your game face on, cause this is gonna be a battle to remember."

"Don't worry," the oldest Townsend sister said. "Noel and I are ready."

"Good because the race starts now!" Wanda shouted and slammed the accelerator to the floor. The cart started slowly, already slipping on the slick grass. Abby's cart shot ahead quickly as Noel used her air magic to help the cart along. The men were just ahead, all of them hunched forward as if that would make Lin's cart go faster.

Magical rain conjured by Clay started to poor down on Wanda's cart, and Faith quickly deflected it with a flick of her wrist, sending it over to Abby's cart and causing her three sisters to get drenched. They shrieked, but it wasn't long before Noel created an air bubble to keep the rain off them. Earth, wind, and water flew around all three carts as each of the witches tried to slow down their competitors. But it quickly became clear to Faith that the regular tactics weren't going to work. They were all powerful and able to create a counter spell to either compensate or deflect. What they needed to do was team up.

She leaned forward. "Hanna, let's bog the men down with a muddy path. Clay won't be able to keep up with both of us."

Hanna's eyes gleamed, and the two witches turned their attention to the men's cart, conjuring a flood of water for the ground just ahead of them. The pool appeared without warning, and the cart splashed into the makeshift pond, water going everywhere as they came to a sudden stop. As they flew by, Faith heard Clay curse and say the wheels were buried in the mud.

Faith held her hand up, and Hanna high-fived her. "Nice!"

Brian leaned in close. His breath was warm on her cheek as he said, "Well played."

"Thanks. Hanna and I make a good team," she said, not minding at all when he pulled her closer to him. She was tucked into the crook of his arm, enjoying that the warmth of his body was protecting her from the ice-cold air Noel was shooting at them.

Abby's cart was a good ten feet in front of them, and Wanda was cursing, saying something about her turbos not working.

"We can't combat this wind," Hanna said. "What do we do?"

Wanda followed Abby around the turnaround point and then glanced back at Brian "Ready?" she asked.

"Absolutely." While still holding Faith with one arm, he lifted the other and traced something in the air, creating a fire outline.

"Is that...?" Faith's eyes widened as she took in the phallic shape dancing in front of her eyes.

"It's a flaming dildo!" Hanna exclaimed.

"What are you doing with that?" Faith asked, her words cracking with her laughter.

"Entertaining your sisters." He winked, traced a few more fire dildos into the air, and then sent the orbs flying toward the lead cart. It was then Faith noticed that Wanda had traced her own fire dildos and sent them after Brian's.

Wanda had somehow managed to gain on Abby, and they were only half a cart length behind. The fire dildos were floating above Abby's cart, seemingly waiting for a command.

"Watch this," she said as she reached down and flipped a switch on the console of the golf cart. The song "I'm Too Sexy" started blaring out of her surround sound. Up ahead, Faith could just make out where the dildos had lined up in front of her sister's cart and started bobbing to the beat of the music.

Abby, Yvette, and Noel started screaming with laughter. Noel raised her hand and sent a gust of air at them, presumably trying to wave away the dancing dildos, but all she managed to do was make them swell, the air fueling the fire.

Faith glanced at Brian. "You'll never live down the fact that you conjured fire penises, you know that, right?"

His eyes gleamed with mischief. "Why would I want to live that down? This story is going to be legendary."

"Oh. Em. Gee!" Hanna pointed off to the right. "Look!"

Faith followed her gaze and jerked back in surprise when

she spotted the men from the other cart bent over, their pants at their ankles as the moon reflected off their backsides.

"I'm so glad I bailed on that cart," Brian said with a small shudder. "Of course, if I'd been with them I wouldn't have the burning desire to scrub my eyeballs with bleach."

"This party is insane," Hanna said, wheezing because she was laughing so hard.

A burst of hilarity erupted from Abby's cart just as Wanda inched by them. Faith was speechless as she watched Yvette blast the fire dildos with a burst of her own fire, causing them to spurt fire as if they were ejaculating right before they winked out and turned to smoke.

The cart jerked to a stop, and Wanda thrust her fist into the air as she yelled, "Yes! We did it! Perfect, Brian. I told you that would distract their pervy butts."

Faith and Hanna stared at each other, both of them with their mouths hanging open. Then Hanna threw her head back and laughed until tears streamed down her face.

Abby, Yvette, and Noel ran over, each of them animated, waving their arms and laughing along with Wanda and Hanna.

"Faith?" Brian asked.

"Yeah?"

"Are you all right?" His dark eyes searched hers. "Is something wrong, or is this just not really your scene?"

Dammit. She mentally kicked herself. Why was she having such a hard time enjoying herself? The evening's events should've left her warm and fuzzy from having a handsome man interested in her. Not to mention that she should be clutching her side and wheezing from laughing too hard, just like Hanna. Instead, she was unsettled and unable to put Hunter and the raven-haired woman out of her mind.

"I'm just tired after a long day," she said, forcing a smile as she watched her sisters and their men run down to the river. She groaned. "Are they doing what I think they're doing?"

"Come on, Faith!" Hanna called, stripping her shirt off. "We're all going for a swim."

"Looks like it." Brian eyed her curiously. "Not interested?"

She should be. There was a gorgeous man sitting next to her who was probably game, but all she wanted to do was crawl into bed. "Not really. I think I'll wait here until they wear themselves out. But you should go join them. I'll be fine."

"Nah. I've got a better idea. Wait here. I'll be right back. Brian slipped out of the cart and headed down to the river. After speaking to Clay, who'd still been standing by the bank, he returned with a self-satisfied smile on his face. He held out a hand to her. "Come on. I'll take you home."

"What? How?" she asked as she let him help her out of the cart.

He held up a key and jerked his head toward Lin's cart that had already been moved to dry ground. "I'll get you home and then come back for my boys."

Faith nearly cried with relief. "You're a lifesaver."

"Yeah? Enough of a lifesaver that you'll let me take you to dinner on Friday?" he asked as they climbed into Lin's cart.

His question caught her off guard, but as she turned to him, that dimple flashed at her again and she heard herself say, "I'd love to."

CHAPTER 5

*H*unter walked around the large barn on Lincoln Townsend's property. A window needed to be changed, more than a few boards had suffered rot, and the roof was leaking. He turned to Lin and said, "Sure, I can get it back into shape. No problem."

"Good," Lin said. "That should keep you busy for a while. After that I could use help with everything from splitting logs to fixing irrigation systems. It's more of a jack-of-all-trades type job, nothing like the high-end work you did for Faith, but if you're game, you're hired."

The luxury spa Hunter had built out for Faith was the kind of thing he really wanted to be doing. The job showed off his skills, and there was a satisfaction in turning a space into something beautiful. But because he'd left town months ago and canceled all his projects, he had to start back up somewhere. Rebuilding a barn wasn't a sexy job, but it was a job working for Lincoln Townsend. The guy was beloved by the town, and if word got out Hunter was working for him, it would do wonders for restoring his reputation. "I'm more than game. If someone wants to hire me for side work, do you have a problem with that?"

"Not at all. Just as long as you show up here when you're supposed to and get the work done, your time is your own," Lin said.

"Perfect. You won't have to worry about that. I take my commitments seriously." Hunter held his hand out to the older man.

Lin grasped Hunter's hand and shook, his grip much firmer than Hunter would've imagined from the frail-looking man. When he let go, he said, "You might need to convince the rest of the town about that last part before they decide to hire you. Miss Maple ended up having to hire someone from out of town to finish that shelving for her, and the Pelshes ended up redoing their floors themselves. People were a little put off."

Hunter nodded, knowing that had to be the case. He'd contacted his clients to let them know he'd been called away on an emergency and apologized, but he hadn't exactly been timely about it. He'd been in too much shock and pain to care. His lack of communication had tanked his business in Keating Hollow. But he was certain it wasn't anything he couldn't recover from. "I understand. They have every right to be skeptical after the way I left this summer, but I'm committed to Keating Hollow now. They'll see."

"And what about Faith?" Lin asked.

Hunter jerked his head up and was so surprised by the question he actually took a step back. "I'm sorry? What do you mean, 'what about Faith?'"

He frowned. "Didn't you agree to do the work for her outdoor space? The fire pit and a rock wall or something?"

Relief rushed through Hunter, realizing he wasn't going to have to explain his intentions regarding Faith with her father. Not that he even knew himself. He just knew he wanted to see her, spend time with her, and somehow get her to give him another chance. "Yes, but I was under the impression it had already been taken care of."

Lin shook his head. "No. When you left she put it on hold. At first she was waiting for you to come back, but then after she interviewed a half-dozen landscape specialists and dismissed them all, she decided to backburner the project until she had time to track down a quality contractor. But now that you're back..." He shrugged. "You might want to make it right."

Hunter ground his teeth together. Why had she told him the work had already been done? She had said the work was done, hadn't she? All he could recall was her saying she didn't have any construction projects at the moment. *Damn*, he thought. She'd meant she hadn't wanted to hire him. Determination settled in his bones as he recalled the plans they'd talked about for the outdoor space. Well, she didn't have to hire him. But that wouldn't stop him from following through on his word. She wasn't likely to stop him if he did the work for free, was she? Not the Faith he knew. The woman who'd put A Touch of Magic together wasn't one to make foolish business decisions. And turning down free labor just because she was annoyed wasn't her style.

"I wasn't aware of that," he said to Lin. "Consider it done. I'll make it a priority to finish the work at her spa and anything else she needs."

"Good." Lincoln shoved his hands in his pockets and nodded to the barn. "I have a tab at the hardware store. I'll call and let Harold know you're doing work for me and to put the supplies on my account. Do you need any special tools?"

Hunter shook his head. "No, sir. My truck is fully stocked."

"Excellent. You can start tomorrow." Lincoln Townsend jumped into his mud-caked golf cart and waved a hand. "Get in. There's berry pie and fresh coffee back at the house."

Hunter's stomach growled at the thought of pie, and he wondered when he'd last eaten. Last night? This morning? A vague memory of scarfing down a slice of toast as he rushed out the door to get Zoey registered that morning floated to the surface. They'd spent all morning at the school, and then Hunter had made a beeline for the Townsend home without stopping for lunch.

"You hungry, McCormick?" Lin asked as he carefully steered the cart around a fallen redwood tree that was blocking the path back to the house.

"Yeah, I guess I am." He glanced back at the redwood. "You want me to clear that tomorrow? It looks like it's been in the way for a while."

"Ever since the storm came through a couple of months ago. They called the gust hurricane force winds. We lost four more way in the back of the orchard, but they can wait. That one," he jerked a thumb over his shoulder, "is getting on my last nerve. If you took care of it, I wouldn't mind."

"Sure. I can even do it today if you want," Hunter said. "Tomorrow I want to get a decent start on the roof before the afternoon weather kicks in, so I'll be here early."

Lin eyed Hunter, nodded, and said, "You're going to work out just fine." He parked the cart near the back door of his log cabin and climbed out. "Come on. Pie first, then we can see about that tree."

HUNTER PARKED his truck a few spaces down from A Touch of Magic. He killed the engine and was about to jump out when his phone buzzed with a text. Vivian... again.

Are you on your way yet? We're waiting for you for dinner.

He sucked in a deep breath and let it out before he texted

back. He'd already told her he'd be late. After pie with Lin, he'd spent the rest of the afternoon clearing the redwood tree. Then he'd gone to the hardware store, stocking up on materials so that he could hit the barn hard first thing in the morning. There was just one more thing to do before he called it a day.

The phone started to ring, and Vivian's name flashed across the screen. Hunter closed his eyes and prayed for patience. "Hello?"

"Oh, good. You're there. Zoey is asking when you'll be home," she said, her tone sounding just as annoyed as he felt.

"Probably an hour or so. I'll be there to read to her and tuck her in." He opened the truck door and stepped out onto Main Street.

"What's taking you so long? I told you I was making dinner. You must be starving by now."

He pulled the phone away from his ear and stared at it for a moment. When had she decided she had say-so over what he did and when he did it? They weren't involved in any way other than caring for Zoey. "Vivian, I already told you I'm busy with work. You do not need to cook for me. I'll be home when I get there. All right?"

"But Zoey—"

"She'll be fine. I have to go." He ended the call, wondering if he'd made a mistake bringing Vivian to Keating Hollow. But how could it be a mistake when he considered Zoey? Vivian was acting as if they were a couple, something he was going to have to talk to her about sooner rather than later.

But at that moment, there was another woman he needed to talk to. One he hadn't been able to get out of his mind for the last year. He paused to take in the vibrant paintings in the front window display and smiled when he realized they were animated. She'd taken his suggestion and had found someone to spell them with subtle movements. One had a woman holding a wilting rose. But as he approached, she blew on it and the petals perked up, reviving the bloom. In the other, a man held an unlit candle. With a wave of his hand, the flame sparked to life, illuminating the words that read: *Treat yourself to a touch of magic.*

Two women strolled out the front door, both of them glowing under the street lamps.

"That was the best massage I've ever had," one of them said with a contented sigh. "The knots in my shoulders are gone, and I feel ten years younger."

"Did you get a sugar scrub?" the other one asked. "My girl used citrus, and I smell so good I want to pour tequila on myself and do body shots."

"I'm not sure that's how that works," her friend said with a laugh.

"I know, and I don't even care!" They were giggling as they moved down the sidewalk toward Incantation Café.

Her shop was a huge success. He'd known it would be. An invisible chime went off as he walked through the door. The soft tinkling music was soothing and complimented the clean lemongrass scent in the air. The reception area was warm, and everything about it was inviting.

A petite Latina woman rose from her chair behind the desk and said, "Hello there. Can I help you?"

"Yes, I'm here to see Faith," he said.

A small crinkle formed on her forehead as she frowned slightly. "Hmm, did you have an appointment, Mr...." she glanced up, waiting for him to supply his name.

"McCormick, and no, I do not have an appointment. If she's busy with a client, I can wait."

"I'm not busy," Faith said. "But we are getting ready to close. Is it important?"

He turned and found her standing in the doorway that led

to the back of the spa. The tension of the day faded away as he took her in. Her gorgeous blond hair was piled on her head in an elegant twist with a few strands framing her face. Her cheeks were rosy, and her eyes were sparking with annoyance. He knew the annoyance was directed at him, and he was looking forward to the challenge of replacing it with pleasure.

Hunter gave her an easy smile. "I think so, yes. Got a few minutes? I'll help you lock up if you're in a hurry."

"Faith," her receptionist said a little too eagerly. "Go ahead. I've got everything covered."

"Lena," Faith said, a warning in her tone. "I can handle this." She turned her attention back to Hunter. "I can give you five minutes." Then she spun and disappeared into the back.

Hunter didn't hesitate. He followed her, already knowing where she'd be heading. He'd spent six months of his life with her. And even though they hadn't had a chance to take their relationship further than a friendly flirtation, now that Craig was gone, she was the only person who he actually felt a connection to. Besides Zoey, of course.

After making his way down the hall, he turned left and pushed the door open to the small kitchen that had been stocked with a variety of healthy snacks and an espresso machine. She was already sitting at the bar, waiting for her espresso to brew. Hunter walked around the counter, reached down, grabbed the box of pastries he'd known would be there, and handed her a maple bar.

She looked at the donut for a moment and then chuckled. "I always forget you know my weaknesses."

"We did work together for six months." He handed her the espresso shot, grabbed a glazed donut, and sat down next to her. "The spa looks fantastic."

"Thanks, but most of that is because of you," she said as she stared into her cup.

"It was your vision. I just hammered the nails."

She turned then and shook her head at him. "Stop being humble. It's not a good look for you."

"No? Well then, how's this? Your outdoor space still hasn't been done. I'm here to let you know I'm going to start work on it this week."

Her amused expression vanished as her eyes flashed with anger. "What? I already told you we weren't in the market for any renovations right now. You should really talk to my dad. He's the one with projects waiting."

"I already did." He waved a hand at his dirt-smudged jeans. "We got a tree cleared, and I start on his barn tomorrow." Leaning forward slightly, he caught her gaze and said, "Faith, I'm not here asking for a job. I'm here to finish the one I started."

Her blue eyes blazed with indignation at first, but as they continued to stare at each other, the mood shifted. Suddenly instead of animosity, there was heat sparking between them, and Hunter had to hold himself back from pulling her to him and kissing her until the fire reflecting back at him blazed out of control.

She blinked, and the spell was broken. After clearing her throat, she said, "We're still building our client base, and there just isn't any money in the budget for the outdoor space right now. Thanks, but maybe another time. Next fall would probably be better." She shrugged. "We'll have to see how the spa is doing."

"Could you afford to supply the materials?" he asked.

"Probably, but that's beside the point." She slid off her chair. "Thanks for coming by, but it's been a long day, and I have an afterhours client coming in that I have to prepare for."

She turned to go, but Hunter reached out and gently

grabbed her wrist, stopping her. "I wasn't going to bill you for my labor, Faith."

She frowned at him. "Why would you do something like that?"

"Because I let you down and I want to make it up to you. I could also use the reference. I'm back for good now and need to rebuild my client base too. Since you're the only one I've done work for in Keating Hollow, I want to make sure your experience is stellar."

Faith just stared at him, her expression unreadable.

He wanted to press his palm to her cheek, pull her in closer, and kiss her until everything else faded away... until the only thing that mattered was being in each other's arms.

"You can't do the work for free," she said, shaking her head. "That's not how I do business."

Her words brought him back to reality, and he rested one elbow on the bar. "You aren't. I'm getting a reference out of it."

She rolled her eyes. "I will give you a reference for the work you did on the spa already. It's not like you ran out on me without finishing the work I contracted you for. You deserve it. The place is beautiful."

"Thanks, but I didn't finish. I told you I'd build the rock wall and fire pit. If you still want those, I'm ready and willing to get them done. It'll only take about a week. It would be shorter, but I've got work for your dad to do as well."

She let out a deep sigh. "Why don't you just get him to provide a reference? His word is gold around here."

"I will, but the work I'm doing for him is mostly manual labor. The work I want to do is design for upscale places. Turning a space from an empty shell into a work of art is what gets me excited. Your place fits that bill to a T."

She pressed her lips into a thin line and glanced away. "I just don't think it's a good idea."

Frustrated that she was fighting him so hard, he stood and took one of her hands in his, holding it gently. "Faith, what's really the problem? The fact that you won't be paying me for the work? Or do you just not want me around?"

He held his breath as he waited for her to answer. He hadn't meant to put her on the spot like that, but the words had just come out. *Well, better to know one way or another,* he thought.

"It's not..." She shook her head. "I don't feel right about not paying you."

Relieved she hadn't told him to scram, he relaxed his shoulders and gave her an easy smile. "How about a trade? I'll do the work for your outdoor space, you pay for the supplies and pay me in services. Massages, scrubs, facials, whatever you think will revitalize this body after flexing my muscles all day."

"You want to take payment in massages?" Her gaze swept over him, and something that looked a lot like desire flashed through her eyes for just a moment. But then she blinked, and it was gone.

"Why not? I'll likely need them."

A slow smile tugged at her lips as she let out a low chuckle. "You're relentless you know that?"

"I am when I want something," he said.

"And a reference is really all you want?" she asked, getting straight to the point.

That right there was one of the things he liked about her most. She was straightforward when she had something to say. He hated games and admired her directness. "I think we both know that isn't true, Faith. Someday soon I'm going to make good on that dinner date we never got to have."

Without saying a word, she pulled her hand out of his and walked to the door. She paused, glanced back and said, "Thank you for your offer to renovate the outdoor space. I'll be sure to mention your commitment to finishing the job in your

46

reference. But don't pursue me, Hunter. From where I'm sitting, your life looks a little crowded."

"Faith, that's not—" he started, but she swept out of the door, letting it close gently behind her.

Dammit. He considered going after her, but what could he say? His life *was* a little crowded, though not in the way that she thought. And he couldn't exactly explain it to her. Not yet anyway. They just both needed some time. After cleaning up the bar where they'd been sitting, he quietly made his way out to the back, and even though the sun had already set, he walked the perimeter and started making notes.

CHAPTER 6

*Y*our client is already waiting for you in the rejuvenation room," Lena said, handing Faith a chart. The young receptionist was staring anxiously at the wall clock, and Faith winced. She'd forgotten Lena had a date.

"Thanks, Lena. I'm sorry if I've made you late. You can take off. I've got it from here."

Relief eased Lena's shoulders as she let out a breath. "I'm not that late yet, but if I hang around here any longer Rhys is probably going to give up on me." She pulled her bag out of a drawer and rushed to the front door. "Tomorrow morning at eight, right?"

"Tomorrow at eight," Faith confirmed as she tried to process the information. Lena had a date with Rhys? The same Rhys who was Clay's assistant at her father's brewery? She bit down on her bottom lip, wondering when that had happened. And should she tell Hanna? Her best friend had been harboring a crush on Rhys for as long as Faith could remember. Finding out he was dating Lena would likely crush her... at least temporarily. Faith would tell her, but she'd do it in person with wine and cookies.

After Lena rushed out, Faith walked to the front door and flipped the sign to closed. On her way to the rejuvenation room, she glanced down at the chart, looking to find out who her mystery client might be.

Brian Knox. The man she had a date with on Friday night.

"Isn't that just perfect," she muttered. Normally she didn't make a habit of massaging men she was dating. There were just too many landmines considering the dynamics. But she couldn't back out. According to his intake form, Brian had made a last-minute appointment, apparently after throwing his back out earlier that day. She couldn't toss him out when she most likely could do something to ease his pain.

When she got to the door of the rejuvenation room, she knocked softly. "Brian, are you ready?"

"Yeah," she heard him grunt out.

She tentatively opened the door and found him wrapped in one of the spa's thick robes, leaning against the massage table.

He glanced at her with a pained expression. "I had trouble getting on the table."

"Oh dear." She put the chart on the counter lining the wall and walked over to him. "I hear you're having some back issues."

He nodded. "I twisted wrong and am pretty sure I pinched a nerve. Now I can barely move."

She scanned his body. "It appears you managed to get undressed at least. That's a start."

Brian let out a huff of humorless laughter. "My clothes are still in a pile on the floor of the men's locker room. I have no idea how I'm going to get redressed."

"Don't worry." She gave him a reassuring smile as all of her trepidation about massaging her date flew out the window. He was in a lot of pain, and there was no way he'd booked this appointment with any romantic intension. The knowledge relaxed her, and she went straight into therapist mode. "I'll fix you up."

"I don't know how you're going to manage that if I can't even lay down on the table," he said and sucked in a sharp breath.

"Hard to breathe, too, huh?" she asked gently as she pulled him away from the table and then pressed the button that lowered it slightly.

"Sometimes if I move wrong." His expression was so pathetic she was torn between feeling sorry for him and laughing.

But as he grimaced, her empathy finally took over and she moved behind him, lightly running her hand over his back. Even through the robe it wasn't hard for her to find the affected muscles. Intense heat radiated from his lower back as if a beacon was calling to her magic.

"Whoa," she said quietly. "You really did a number on yourself, didn't you?"

"I was watching Skye for Jacob and Yvette, and when I reached down to pick her up off the floor where she'd been playing, my back seized. The next thing I knew I was on the ground with her as she laughed at me."

"You forgot to bend your knees," she said with a gentle smile.

"I'm getting old is the problem. No one tells you that once you turn thirty things start to fall apart."

She couldn't help it. She laughed. "Is that it? Over the hill at the ripe age of thirty? We better get you a walker."

"I'm thirty-five, and right about now a walker sounds like the perfect solution," he said with a huff.

"Thirty-five, that *is* old," she teased. "But let's not place the order for the walker just yet, okay? Let me see what I can do first." She lifted the top sheet off the table. "Go ahead and sit if you can. If not, you can use me for support."

"I can do that much," he said and winced as he bent his knees just enough so that he was sitting on the edge of the table.

"Good. Can you scoot back a bit?"

He did as she asked, gritting his teeth with the movement.

"Excellent. Now I'm going to help you lie on your shoulder. From there, we'll get you on your stomach so I can get to work."

Faith had done this before. And because Brian was determined to have her work on him, he did as she asked without too much resistance. But it didn't take a witch to understand that he was in a lot of pain. His face was red with the effort, and every muscle was tensed and overcompensating for his back injury. Still, she managed to get him on his stomach and, with a little bit of care, out of his robe. It was all she could do to keep from staring at his perfect butt.

Geez, she thought as she covered him with a sheet and couldn't help the glimpse of his perfect backside. Gods, he was beautiful. She just couldn't understand why she couldn't be more attracted to him instead of Hunter. Maybe she just needed time. Didn't people say that friends to lovers made the best kinds of lasting relationships? But she and Hunter would be friends to lovers as well.

"Faith?" he asked.

"Huh?" She glanced down at him lying on her table, the sheet covering his lower half. His head was turned in her direction and he was studying her.

"Where did you go? Seems like you were miles away there for a second."

She swallowed a nervous laugh. She could hardly tell him

she'd been wishing that he turned her on. "I was just working out the best way to ease your pain."

Total lie. She already knew what to do.

"You think you can do it?" he asked.

"Absolutely." She grabbed a bottle of the healing lotion her sister Abby had brewed for her and squeezed a dollop into her hand. "I've been told my hands are magic."

"So I've heard. When I called the healers here in town, Gerry told me my best bet was to come see you. She said most likely she'd just refer me to you anyway. She said we'd talk about pain management only if you couldn't help."

Gerry Whipple and her husband Martin were the town healers. And like most witches, they preferred their clients try holistic remedies before they prescribed any kind of pain medication. "I think you'll be pleasantly surprised by the time we're done here. Now just relax while I get to work. Let me know if you need me to adjust the pressure at any time."

"Okay. Try not to hurt me."

Faith chuckled. "I'll do my best."

When she'd been younger, Faith had always thought herself a somewhat mediocre witch. Her three sisters had come into their powers fairly easily and wielded their elements with ease. But Faith, the water witch of the family, hadn't ever been super comfortable wielding water. She could do it, but the element rarely did exactly what she asked it to. She could manipulate water, but getting her spells to last any length of time was futile. It wasn't until she studied to be a massage therapist that she'd come into her own.

Something had happened the first time she'd laid her hands on one of her school mates. As she was working her muscles, she realized she had a sense of what the body needed to heal. It wasn't that she could manipulate the body's fluids, it was just that she could see in her mind what the issues were, and it allowed her to find and work through the problem areas with great effectiveness.

Faith took her time running her hands over Brian's back, starting with his upper back and moving downward. He'd definitely aggravated a muscle and pinched a nerve, but it wasn't just his lower back. The guy was tight everywhere, which likely contributed to his injury.

"Brian," she said softly, "you have a lot of tension. Is this new?"

"No, but it's worse than usual." He let out a small grunt as she kneaded the muscles around his shoulder blades.

"Have you changed your routine? Doing something different?" Pressing both hands flat on his back, she used her weight to apply pressure and slid her hands slowly down to his lower back, just trying to help him relax before she really got to work.

"You could say that. I'm building a house not too far from Jacob's."

"Oh, wow. That would do it. Okay then, looks like I have some work to do." She reached over and hit the play button on her music dock. The calming music filled the room as Faith's magic tingled at her fingertips. Then she got lost in her work as she homed in on the irritated muscle that was the source of Brian's problem.

An hour later, her arms and fingers fatigued from a job well done, she pulled the sheet over Brian and said, "I left you some water on the counter. Take your time getting up, and when you're ready, I'll meet you out front."

"Gods, Faith, you're a lifesaver," Brian said with a contented sigh. "You saved me from a sleepless night of self-medicating. Thank you."

She smiled down at him. "Any time, Brian. Glad I could help."

Fifteen minutes later, Brian strolled out of the back room, a look of complete bliss on his face.

"Hello there," she said. "You look a thousand times better than you did when I found you leaning against the massage table."

"I *am* a thousand times better, thanks to you." He pulled out some bills and pushed them across the front desk. "You're pure magic, Faith Townsend."

She eyed the bills without picking them up. "That's way too much, Brian. It's double the price of the service."

"You deserve it," he said as he shoved his wallet in his back pocket. "You saved my ass, literally."

She picked up the bills and pushed a few of them back toward him. "It's what you pay for. Take that and get yourself some dinner or something."

He eyed the bills, frowning. "Only if you come with me."

She glanced at the clock. It was already past seven and she needed to be in the office early in the morning. Plus, she'd just spent the last eighty minutes touching his naked body. Going on a sort-of date didn't seem like the most responsible move. She gave him a half-hearted smile and said, "I can't tonight. But thanks for the offer. Besides, you should go rest your back and rehydrate. You don't want to reinjure yourself."

"We both have to eat," he pressed. "Come on, Faith. I'm going to the Cozy Cave either way."

Right then her stomach growled, and her cheeks heated with embarrassment.

"Ah, see! You are hungry. Come on, Faith. You need food."

"Oh, all right. But just dinner, then I have to get home." She stuffed his bills into the register, grabbed her coat, and met him at the front door.

"Are you implying my intensions are less than honorable?" he asked.

"Brian, you asked if I wanted to share the massage table with you right after I finished your massage. You're not an innocent." She held the door open for him and then followed him out into the street.

"Hey, it was comfortable," he said with mock chasteness.

"I bet." She snorted and pulled her keys out of her jacket pocket.

As she was locking the door, Brian bent down and picked something up. "Hey, Faith, you dropped this."

She turned and spotted the letter she'd shoved in her pocket the night before. The one that didn't have a return address. "Thanks. I forgot all about that." She took it and tore it open, thinking it was probably an advertisement or a charity asking for a donation. But when she pulled it out, she scanned the handwritten letter and then let out a gasp when she saw the signature.

"What is it?" Brian asked. "Bad news?"

She glanced up at him, pure shock rooting her in place. "No. It's from my mother."

CHAPTER 7

"Uncle Hunter, Uncle Hunter," Zoey called as she ran through the house. "Mommy made us breakfast."

Hunter sat at his desk that he'd relocated to the living room when he'd moved Vivian and Zoey in. He'd gotten up early and had started working on designs for Faith's outdoor sanctuary. He sat back as the little girl came running around the corner, her dark hair flying behind her. Joy swelled his heart as she jumped into his lap, wrapping her arms around his neck.

"She made waffles," Zoey said, beaming up at him. Her dark eyes sparkled with happiness, something he hadn't seen much of since Craig had passed.

"It looks like you're excited about that," he said, wrapping her in his arms as he stood and carried her into the kitchen.

Vivian, who was dressed up in a fashionable tailored suit, was wearing an apron and standing at the table, filling two coffee cups. The table was set, and each plate had a waffle already placed in the middle. She'd also made bacon, scrambled eggs, and toast.

Hunter placed Zoey in a chair and stared at Vivian in surprise. "You cooked up a storm."

"Of course I did. Zoey needs fuel before school, so I made enough for everyone." She smiled serenely and sat next to her daughter.

Hunter glanced around at the elaborate spread, wondering if she'd cooked like this before Craig's accident. He'd stayed with them for five months in Las Vegas and hadn't seen her do more than make grilled cheese. Hunter had been the one who'd cooked for them. It had been the least he could do while she dealt with the loss of her husband.

"Thanks." He sat and tucked in, eating a double helping of everything. Construction burned a lot of calories, and he had room to spare. After he decimated everything on his plate, he leaned back in his chair and sipped at his coffee. "This was great. Thanks, Viv."

"You're very welcome." She leaned over to Zoey and said, "Go get your backpack, sweetie. It's almost time to leave for school."

Zoey slid out of her chair and ran into the bedroom she shared with her mother.

Vivian smoothed her dark hair back and sent Hunter a contented smile. "It feels good to be cooking for my family again. I haven't felt this normal in months."

"That's... good." He hadn't missed her words, *my family*. She was including him in that tidy little picture, not just Zoey, and he wasn't sure what to do with that. He was well aware that she'd like to start a relationship with him and have him step right into Craig's shoes, but while Hunter was more than willing to do whatever it took to care for them, he was never going to hook up with Vivian again. A romantic relationship was the last thing he wanted with her. There was a reason they'd broken up all those years ago. He chose to ignore her insinuation and said, "You look nice. Are you job hunting today?"

She set her cup on the table and nodded. "I feel overdressed, but it's either this or a skirt, and there's snow in the forecast. I don't want to get caught walking around town with bare legs."

"Snow?" he asked, already turning to glance out the window. The day was drizzly and gray with just a peek of the sun spilling over his immaculate lawn.

"Just a dusting, but still. I didn't want to risk it." She stood up and started to clear the table.

He reached over and lightly grabbed her hand, stopping her. "Relax. I've got cleanup. It's the least I can do."

Her expression mellowed, and he was reminded of why he'd been attracted to her all those years ago. There was a softness she kept hidden underneath her tough shell that only a select few ever got to see. When she revealed it, she had the ability to make a man feel like he was her world. Only he also remembered that she'd used that ability to manipulate him into doing things he didn't want to do. She'd wanted him to go to work for a corporation and invest in her father's business. She'd had no respect for his desire to be a self-employed general contractor. In fact, he'd always gotten the impression she thought his job was beneath her.

Craig Chambers had been the perfect husband for her. He'd gone to work in her father's software company as an account manager in sales. By all accounts, he'd been good at it, but then her father's company ran into trouble, and he'd had to sell. Craig was laid off in the process, and ten months later he was gone due to the accident.

It had been a rough time for their family, and between living off their savings and the hospital bills after Craig died, Vivian had been left with nothing but the equity in their house.

It wasn't a lot, but it was enough to start over. He just hoped she'd be ready to move on sooner rather than later.

Because whatever she thought she wanted with him, what she had to offer wasn't the kind of relationship he wanted. He wanted a partner who accepted him as he was and supported his dreams without judgement. Vivian wasn't that woman. She'd always long for more, even if she convinced herself she was happy with a simple life. He just hoped when she moved on that she'd stay close by so he could be in Zoey's life.

"Thank you," she said softly. "See, we make a good team."

He let go of her hand and without saying a word and went to work on the dishes.

"Uncle Hunter," Zoey said, tugging on his hand. "You have to come in and see my new class. It's amazing!"

Hunter chuckled and let the little girl drag him into the school. It was Zoey's second day, and she loved it. It was different than her Las Vegas school, since the one in Keating Hollow also had a curriculum for learning how to control one's magic. That wasn't the case in most places, but since Keating Hollow was a town that was settled by witches over a hundred years ago, it was a tradition that hadn't been phased out by budget cuts or politics.

"Zoey!" A petite little girl with brown curls ran up to her and grabbed her other hand.

"Hi, Daisy. This is my uncle Hunter," Zoey said, pointing to him.

"Hello," the little girl said politely. She quickly turned to Zoey. "You're late. We need to hurry or we're going to miss it!"

"It's the lighting of the school Christmas tree!" Zoey called over her shoulder as the two ran off to the open space in the center of the school.

Hunter chuckled as he followed along behind them, loving that she'd already made a friend. If Zoey managed to settle in painlessly, it was less likely that Vivian would move her again in the short term.

School children were lined up in a circle around a massive blue spruce Christmas tree. Four teachers stood nearby, wands in their hands.

Wands? Since when did the Keating Hollow witches use wands? He heard the clatter of high heels behind him and turned to find Vivian doing her catwalk impersonation down the hallway toward him. She didn't look like anyone who lived or worked in Keating Hollow. She was far too made up. From the sexy suit, to the heels, to the make-up, she was about ten beauty steps ahead of everyone else. Yes, she was gorgeous, but she also looked like she was trying too hard.

"Did you know this school uses wands? Isn't that a little dangerous for kids?" he asked her when she came to a stop beside him. Wands carried power and ancient spells. The last thing the kids needed was another child unleashing a power spell he or she had no skill to control.

"It's just for show and to help them concentrate. Don't worry, I already asked about them. No one is going to turn Zoey into a unicorn. Although she might actually like that," Vivian said with a chuckle.

Hunter crossed his arms over his chest and watched as the four teachers waved their wands and in unison said, "From the gifts of our elements, we ask that the gods bless us with the trimming of the tree."

The students all repeated the phrase.

Silence filled the chilled air. It was so quiet Hunter was half positive that a teacher had cast a charm over the kids. But then a bird chirped, and the teachers started waving their wands around. A bottle of water rose in the air and tilted, and water started to pour out. Before it could reach the ground one of the teachers flicked her wrist, and the water rose into the air, separated, and reformed into two dozen icicles. Another flick of the wrist and the icicles each found a place on the tree. Each teacher used their element to decorate the tree, and in no time, the tree was filled with magical flames flickering on white candles, blooming poinsettias that had no need to be watered, and miniature fake swans that had become animated and were now perched on the branches.

The kids squealed and cheered as they were herded to their classrooms. Zoey ran over to Hunter and Vivian, gave them each a big hug and a kiss on the cheek, and then ran back to her classmates, who were already filing into a nearby classroom.

Hunter placed a hand on the small of Vivian's back and guided her toward the school entrance. "She seems to love it here."

Vivian nodded. "At least that's one thing that's going right."

"Mr. and Mrs. McCormick!" the woman Hunter recognized as the principal called and hurried over to them.

"We're not—" Hunter started to say that they weren't married and that in fact, Vivian and Zoey didn't share his last name, but Vivian cut him off.

"Hello, Janice. The tree lighting was perfect," Vivian said.

"Thank you. It's a favorite every year. I just wanted to tell you both how much we love having Zoey. She's a delightful child. She's already made fast friends with Daisy, the daughter of Noel Townsend. Good people the Townsends." She grinned at Hunter. "But you already know that, right? I heard you're doing work for Lin. Such a great guy."

"Yes, he is," Hunter said.

"Anyway. I have to run. Let us know if there's anything we can do to make the settling-in process smoother for Zoey." The principal waved her fingers at them and strode off.

"That was certainly nice," Vivian said as they walked back out to his truck.

Hunter was quiet as he held the door open for her. The interaction had disturbed him. Why had the principal called them Mr. and Mrs. McCormick? He continued to stew about the interaction as he put the truck in gear and headed to the heart of the town. Finally, he couldn't stand it and just asked her. "Viv, why does the principal think we're married?"

"Oh, that." She waved an unconcerned hand. "When I filled out Zoey's paperwork, I used your last name. I figured it would just be easier than changing it later."

He pulled the truck into a parking spot on Main Street and stared at her in confusion. "What are you talking about? Why would you do that?"

"You know why," she said, impatiently. "Come on, Hunter. Give me a break, will you? I'm just trying to do the right thing."

"By erasing Craig completely?" he roared and then shot out of the truck, needing the fresh air to cool his temper. Craig didn't deserve what she was doing to him. He'd been Zoey's father for seven years of her life. She couldn't just erase that because it made life easier for her.

"Hunter, please," she said, standing beside the truck with her arms crossed over her chest in a protective stance. "This is hard enough as it is. I was just trying to... I don't know. It seemed like the right thing to do. We're sort of like a family now. And if we just give it time..." Her voice wobbled, and she glanced away, but not before he noticed the tears in her eyes.

He let out a frustrated sigh and took a deep breath, trying to calm himself. Walking over to her, he used two fingers to lift her face so that she was looking up at him. "Viv, you can't just change things like that. Don't you think it's too confusing for Zoey? She's been a Chambers her entire life. She can't just switch to McCormick out of nowhere."

"She's happy to be a McCormick," Viv said as a single tear rolled down her face. "Craig would understand."

Hunter highly doubted that. In fact, he was fairly certain his friend was rolling in his grave right at that moment. A sharp stab of pain sluiced through him even as his heart seemed to swell with the idea. He couldn't let her do this. It wasn't fair to Craig or Zoey.

"Vivian, listen, you have to go back to the school and make sure they know that Zoey's last name is Chambers. It's her legal name, and we aren't married, nor will we ever be. You have to stop thinking you can will things into existence."

"Why are you fighting this?" she asked, her eyes searching his in earnest. "Craig is gone. You aren't betraying him, and Zoey deserves to have a father."

Hunter ground his teeth together, praying for patience. "Zoey has a father!" he said through clenched teeth, wanting to shake her. "You know I'm committed to her, that I'm not going anywhere, but Craig deserves to live in her memory and you're trying to erase him. I won't let you do it."

"I'm not trying to erase him," she said very quietly. "I'm just trying to do the right thing for my daughter."

"So am I," he said, closing his eyes, trying to regain control. "But you have to stop forcing this, Vivian. You and me, we're never going to end up together the way you want us to. I'm not... it's just not what I'm looking for."

"You mean *I'm* not what you're looking for," she said with a huff of irritation.

It was true, but he hadn't wanted to come out and just say it like that. Finally, he opted for the truth. "I'm sorry, Viv. The fact is that I'm interested in someone else."

"It's Faith, isn't it? The pretty blonde you were talking to at the bookstore. She owns the spa, doesn't she?" Her words were matter-of-fact, void of emotion.

He didn't even acknowledge her question. Instead, he bent down and kissed her softly on the cheek. "I'm sorry, Viv. Please talk to the school so there aren't any more miscommunications. I have to get to work." He climbed back into his truck, rolled down the window, and said, "Call me if you need a ride home later."

She glared at him. "Don't worry about us. I'll figure something out."

"Okay. Offer stands," he called, pretending she wasn't trying to burn holes in his skull. Then he took off down the road, heading to Lincoln Townsend's farm.

CHAPTER 8

Faith sat at a corner table way in the back of Incantation Café, clutching the letter her mother had sent her. She'd read it at least two dozen times, but she couldn't seem to fully process the words scrawled across the page and read it again, wishing that mother-daughter connection would spring to life. It didn't. How could it? Faith hadn't seen or heard from her mother in twenty-one years.

Her mother had walked out on the family when Faith was only five years old, but she remembered that fall day as if it were just yesterday. Gabrielle Townsend had been a beautiful woman. She had thick honey-blond hair, ocean blue eyes, and an ethereal quality that made Faith remember her as if she were some sort of angel.

Even though the day had been Abby's birthday, it had started out as any other, except their mother had been dressed in sweat pants and a stained sweatshirt instead of her usual chic jeans and flowy blouses. Normally on birthdays, their mother would bring the birthday girl cake in bed. But that morning Gabrielle appeared to have forgotten, and no one even wished Abby a happy birthday.

Yvette had been the one to force the girls into the car and remind their mother to drive them to school. Noel was mad about something, and she and Yvette had argued the entire way to school while their mother, who usually didn't tolerate any nonsense, had ignored their bickering. By the time Gabby dropped them off, Faith's ears had been ringing from the screaming.

Faith remembered standing on the sidewalk with Abby as they watched the old Volvo disappear down the street. Faith had been unsettled but hadn't realized it at the time. All she knew was that she desperately wanted to be back at home, cuddled up next to her mother.

Two hours later, Faith burst into tears and demanded that the nurse call her mother. She had to see her. Had to go home.

When no one had been able to calm Faith, they'd done as she asked and called Gabby to come get her, thinking maybe she was coming down with something.

But no one answered, and Gabby hadn't come for Faith. It was her dad, Lin, who'd arrived an hour later and scooped his daughter up into his arms. He'd wiped her tears away and taken her home. Faith had run into the house looking everywhere for her mother, but she was nowhere to be found. It was then that Faith had the dreaded feeling that she'd never see her mother again. She'd known before Lin found her mother's empty closet and the empty bank account. Before Abby had come home and found out her mother had abandoned her on her birthday.

Gabrielle Townsend had left them without a word or any hint that she was leaving. But five-year-old Faith had some sort of premonition that day at school, and she'd been the only one who knew without a doubt that her mother wasn't coming back.

Twenty-one years later, Faith had been wholly unprepared for her mother's letter. She'd let that relationship go a long time ago, but now it was all she could think about. Her mother had written her. She knew where her youngest daughter lived, and she wanted to reconnect. Wanted to mend fences.

Faith had no idea what to do.

"Hey, you," Hanna said, sliding into the seat opposite Faith. She handed her a mocha latte with extra whip. "What's wrong? You look like someone stole your puppy."

"No one would steal Xena. She's a terror wrapped up in a ball of fluff," Faith said. "If they did, they'd return her within the hour."

Hanna snickered then stuck her bottom lip out in an exaggerated pout. "Poor Xena. She just needs to grow up a little bit. I bet she turns into a great dog."

"That's what I keep praying for." Faith slid the letter in her hand over to Hanna. "This came in the mail a few days ago."

Hanna picked it up, glanced at it and gasped. "Holy balls, Faith. Is this really from your mom?"

"That's what it says." She blew out a breath and buried her face in her hands. "I don't know what to do with that."

There was silence between them as Hanna read the letter. When she was done, she put the letter down on the table and smoothed out the crinkles from where Faith had clutched the paper.

"Well?" Faith asked. "What do you think I should do?"

"She's your mom, Faith. I think you kinda have to respond." She glanced down at the letter again. "Have you told your sisters?"

Faith shook her head. "Not yet. I don't know what to say. How do you tell your sisters that your mother wrote you a letter and asked you not to tell them you heard from her? Besides, I want to have a pretty good idea of what I want to do before I talk to them. I don't want anyone trying to make up my mind for me. You know?"

In the letter, Gabby had written that she wanted to make contact with each of her girls separately and asked that Faith not tell her sisters that they'd been in contact. Faith was not comfortable with the request at all. Before she did anything, she'd be having a conversation with her sisters and her dad.

"Makes sense," Hanna said. "It's an unreasonable request anyway. Anyone who knows the Townsends sisters knows that you four stick together."

"We do now that Abby is home at least," Faith said. Abby had moved away after high school graduation and stayed away for about a decade. While Faith and Yvette had kept in touch with her, Abby and Noel had suffered some issues. But the four were close now, and hiding this from them was not an option. "Do you really think I have to call her?"

"If you don't, will you regret it?"

Faith closed her eyes and tried to ignore the ache in her gut. It was no use. She knew her answer. "Yes. I'd always wonder."

Hanna reached out and covered Faith's hand with her own. "I know this has to be gut-wrenching for you. But you'll tell your family, and you guys will get through it together."

"What if she's not who I remember?"

Hanna gave her a grim smile. "Sweetie, it's been twenty years. She's definitely not who you remember."

"Ugh. You're right. I mean, what if she's not a nice person? You know, one of those people who hates kids and posts hateful memes on Facebook all day?"

Hanna chuckled. "You'll just block her and move on like everyone else."

"Yeah. But what if it isn't obvious? What if we meet her and she seems fine, but suddenly we find out she's just here for money or to manipulate us or something? I don't know, Hanna. I don't have a great feeling about this." If there was one thing Faith had learned when her mother left all those years ago, it was to trust her gut.

"Oh, sweetie. I know this is hard," Hanna said. "You'll either let her back into your life or you won't, but remember, *you* have all the power here. Don't be afraid to set boundaries. She's the one who left you all, remember? If it turns out she can't earn your trust, you don't have to have a relationship with her."

"You're right." Faith leaned back in her chair. "The first step is to call a family meeting, huh?"

But Hanna didn't answer. She was busy staring out the window.

"What is it?" Faith leaned forward, following Hanna's line of sight.

"Hunter and his girlfriend," she said. "Wow, looks like they're having a row."

"He swears they aren't dating," Faith said as she watched Hunter scowl at Vivian. They exchanged words, but then Hunter seemed to soften a bit as he spoke to her and bent his head to kiss her on the cheek. "I guess that's a lie." Faith sat back in her chair and crossed her arms over her chest. "Why are men such pigs?"

"Oh, come on now. They aren't all terrible," Hanna said, eyeing her friend. "Your sisters seem to have done okay for themselves."

Faith let out a bark of laughter. "It only took them each about ten years and a few really bad apples to get it right." Yvette's marriage had failed when her husband realized he was gay. Noel's first husband had walked out one day and didn't return for six years. And Abby had left town right after graduation, leaving behind the man she loved, because she hadn't been able to deal with the fact that she might've played an accidental role in the tragic death of her best friend Charlotte. "I'd like to do a little better on my first try than they have."

"You just need to pick someone who won't let you down. What about Brian? He seems totally into you. Don't you two have a date on Friday?"

Faith nodded.

"That's a good thing, right?" Hanna picked up her cup and took a long sip of coffee.

"I guess." Faith slumped, hating that she wasn't more excited about dating Brian. If the date wasn't exceptional, she'd have to tell him they could only be friends. She didn't want to lead him on when she was so clearly into someone else. Someone who was clearly taken, no matter what he said. "I just wish I liked him more, you know?"

Hanna nodded, her expression serious. "Like how I like Rhys." She sighed. "Why can't that man see what's right in front of him? I practically threw myself at him the other night. And you know what he did?"

Faith sat up, happy to be hearing about someone else's drama. "He thought you were joking?" It was how he handled everyone who flirted with him while he was working at the brewery.

"Ha! If only. When I told him I was free on Saturday night and looking for a dance partner, he told me to sign up for Magical Connections. Apparently, it's a dating site for witches. Can you believe that? I was wearing that dress that stops traffic, and he told me to sign up for an internet dating site. Is he blind? Am I the annoying little sister type? I don't get it!"

"Oh, honey. No. That's not it at all," Faith said, kicking

herself for not telling her sooner. "It's not you. I think he's dating Lena, my receptionist at the spa."

"Lena? Really?" Hanna's eyes were wide, and she looked perplexed at this new information. "But... he told me a couple of weeks ago he wasn't dating anyone. When did that happen?"

Faith shrugged. "I don't know exactly, but Lena was meeting him last night for a date. I was going to tell you today, but I got distracted by mom stuff. I'm sorry."

"Well..." She stood and threw her shoulders back. "This is good news then."

"Why?"

"Because that means my traffic-stopping dress is not defective. He's just unavailable at the moment. That's fine." She gave Faith a devious smile. "I'll just up my game."

"But if he's dating someone already—" Faith started.

Hanna waved a dismissive hand. "He told me two weeks ago that he was single. If they just started dating, then this isn't serious. I still have time. Just you wait and see what I show up wearing to the pub tonight." She grinned down at Faith. "Wanna join me?"

"Of course. I wouldn't miss this for the world." Faith stood and wrapped her arms around her friend, hugging her tightly. "Thanks for listening. I really needed this."

"Any time, bestie." She let go and leaned back. "Now, go see your sisters. I think once you tell them, you'll feel a thousand times better."

"You're right. I will." Faith followed her to the counter, filched a cookie from the case, and waved at Mary, Hanna's mother. Then she pulled out her phone and called her father. He deserved to be the first one to find out Gabrielle was about to walk back into their lives.

CHAPTER 9

*F*aith stepped out of Incantation Café just as snowflakes started to dust the ground. She held her hands palms up and twirled in delight.

"Who knew it snowed in Keating Hollow?" a familiar male voice asked from behind her.

She turned around, finding Brian strolling toward her, his face lit up in an amused smile. "It's not normal, but it's been known to happen now and then." She returned his smile. "What are you doing out here? Headed for coffee?"

He shook his head. "No, I was coming to see you, actually."

"Oh? At the spa?"

"Yep. Is that where you're headed?" he asked.

She narrowed her eyes and studied him. "Is it your back? Do you need another massage?"

"I'd love one, actually, but only because it was amazing." He reached out and grabbed one of her hands. "You're a miracle worker. It's like there was never a problem. I woke up this morning with more energy than I've had in months."

All of the stress of the morning seemed to vanish with his

praise. That was the reason why she'd chosen massage therapy as a profession. She loved that she could vastly improve another person's quality of life with just a little bit of care and attention. *Magic too,* she reminded herself, but she hadn't known that when she'd chosen her career. "That's what I like to hear. Call Lena for another appointment, even if it's just for maintenance. Building a house is no joke."

"I will. But later. Right now I need your help picking out flooring." He tugged her along Main Street, away from the café and her spa.

"What?" she laughed. "Why? Can't you just pick something yourself?"

He shook his head. "No. I can't. And that spa of yours... it's beautiful, Faith. I need your help. Come on, help a guy out before I pick a patchwork vinyl faux stone that will clash with everything from my kitchen counters to the red leather couch."

"Red leather?" She raised both her eyebrows. "Are you going for the ultimate bachelor pad?"

"See, I need serious help. Save me from myself, Faith. Save me from eternal bachelorhood due to poor decorating."

She rolled her eyes but was seriously amused by his antics. "Fine. Let's go pick your floors. But no arguing, got it? If you pick something not on my approved list, I'm out of there."

"Really? I don't get to have an opinion?" he asked, sounding skeptical.

"Sure you do. But if you're not interested in my advice, then why do I have to be there?"

He laughed. "Fair enough. Let's do this then."

"Let's," she said, her mood lifted. *Is this what it's supposed to feel like when you start dating someone? Comfortable? Fun? Easy?* She had to admit, it didn't suck. The wind picked up and she slipped her arm through his, snuggling into him for his warmth.

He glanced down at her, his lips curved into a small self-satisfied smile. "I like this."

"Yeah?" She tightened her hold on his arm. "You know what, Brian? So do I."

~

FAITH SAT at her desk back at the spa, going over the monthly numbers. Revenue was up. Their appointments were up twenty-five percent. If they continued to grow at the current rate, she was going to need to hire another therapist. *Wouldn't that be nice,* she thought. Then her schedule could be a little more flexible. She'd have more time to spend with Brian if she wanted to.

The only problem was she wasn't sure if she did. It wasn't that she didn't like him. She did, very much. It was just that he seemed to be more into her than she was into him. They'd had a really good time picking out his flooring and then some tiles and paint colors. They'd been silly and shared plenty of laughs, while mostly agreeing on what would look best in his house.

After they were finished, Brian walked her back to the spa. As they stood out front, he'd pulled her close to him and bent his head for a kiss. But before his lips could land on hers, she'd instinctively jerked her head to the side, and he'd awkwardly planted a kiss on her jaw. He'd laughed it off, but she hadn't. She'd been embarrassed and frustrated that she hadn't wanted to kiss him. What was wrong with her? He was gorgeous and fun and a real catch.

The man ran a successful online spa supply business. It was something he fell into after helping his ex-girlfriend shutter her luxury spa business over six months ago. She'd gotten sick and had to let it go, but while it was up and running, he'd done most of the day to day management. He'd learned a lot during his time there, and in what seemed like no time at all, he got his wholesale supply store online. It was already thriving.

She just couldn't figure out why she wasn't attracted to him. Was there something wrong with her? She sighed and put her pen down. They were still on for dinner on Friday, but she was seriously considering cancelling. She didn't want to lead him on if she was never going to reciprocate his obvious feelings for her.

A faint knock sounded at her door, and she stood, fully expecting to be summoned for a late-afternoon appointment. It wasn't unusual for clients to drop in after work, and she'd made a point of being available as she tried to build their client list. She walked over to the door and pulled it open.

"You're not Lena," she said breathlessly as she stared at Hunter and tried not to drool. Holy witches on a broom. The man was scorching hot in his low-slung jeans, black T-shirt that was molded to his muscular chest, and the well-used tool belt around his waist.

"No, I'm definitely not. Got a minute?" he asked as he stepped inside, forcing her back into the depths of her office.

"Sure." She sucked in a calming breath and leaned against her desk, trying to act like she hadn't just been hit over the head with a lust hammer. "What's up?"

He raised his hand and showed her a couple of stone tiles she hadn't noticed he'd been holding. "I need to know which one of these you prefer."

"Oh, right." She took them from him and laid them on her desk. One was slate gray with a marble of lighter gray running through it while the other was a dark brick red with shades of orange and yellow. "Is this for the patio?"

He shook his head. "It's for the bench and fire pit. I thought we'd use something a little subtler for the patio for contrast, but I want you to pick the fire pit first since it will be the showcase of the space."

"Right." She stared down at the tiles, already knowing which one she liked best but wanting his input. On more than one occasion, he'd saved her from making a mistake when he pointed out potential issues with her design choices. "Which do you like?"

He moved to stand next to her and placed his hand on the red tile. "This one compliments the redwoods, but it isn't quite as modern as the classic slate. It depends on who your target audience is. Artsy, nature lovers or city folks who prefer clean lines and minimal distraction."

She smiled up at him. "That's not an opinion, Hunter."

He chuckled. "You're right. It's not."

They stared into each other's eyes, and for Faith time seemed to stop. Electric energy crackled between them, and before she knew what she was doing, she pressed her hand to his stubbled jaw and leaned in.

Her lips brushed over his, and he whispered, "Faith," just before his arms came around her waist and he pulled her into him.

She was lost. His heat, his touch, the scruff of his unshaven jaw, it all overwhelmed her, and desire took over. This was what she'd been waiting for since the night he'd left Keating Hollow five months ago. All she'd wanted was to be in his arms and feel *this* again.

The kiss was tentative, gentle at first, but then she parted her lips, inviting him in. Passion took over as he deepened the kiss, bowing her back slightly, tasting, teasing, and devouring.

"Faith! Someone named Vivian is here to see you," Lena called just as the door swung open. "Oh! Oops. Sorry, I'll come back."

The door slammed shut, and Faith, still in Hunter's arms, stared up at him, shock rendering her speechless.

He grinned down at her. "That was unexpected."

The sound of his voice snapped her out of her silence, and she gently pushed him back, needing to reclaim her personal space. "I'm sorry. That was… I shouldn't have done that."

He frowned. "Why not?"

She waved a hand at the door then between them. "You're working for me and… what about Vivian? And why is she here to see me?"

Hunter glanced once at the closed door then turned his attention back to her. "First of all, I'm not working *for* you. I'm just doing a friend a favor. Second, what about Vivian? It's none of her business who I choose to spend my time with. And it's really none of her business who I'm kissing." His lips twitched into a tiny smile as he gazed down at her. "As for why she's here, I'd guess she's looking to see if you need a sales rep of any kind. She's out pounding the pavement, looking to build her client base."

Faith sat down on the edge of her desk, trying to get her bearings. That kiss had seriously rattled her brain. And she couldn't even blame him. She'd been the one to make the first move. What had she been thinking? Nothing. She hadn't been thinking at all. That was the problem. She cleared her throat. "How can it not be any of her business? You're living together."

He pressed his lips into a tight line and shook his head. "We're sharing a house, sleeping in separate bedrooms. Faith, she was my best friend's wife. I'm just helping them until Vivian gets back on her feet. There's nothing going on there. I swear."

Relief flooded through her, making her slightly light headed. Thank the gods she hadn't just become the other woman. Faith wasn't interested in sharing anyone's man. But then she remembered the fight she'd witnessed on the street earlier in the day and the kiss. Although, the kiss had just been on the cheek. "You're sure? I um... I saw you two this morning outside of Incantation Café. It looked like you were fighting and then making up."

He slumped down into a chair opposite her and ran a hand through his thick dark hair. The frustration rolling off him filled the room, making her shift uncomfortably. He hung his head for a moment. When he finally met her gaze again, he had a look of pure determination and said, "Listen, normally I wouldn't air any of this drama, because on my end it's nothing. Really. But there's something going on here between us, and I don't want to sabotage it by not being completely honest."

Fear coiled deep in her belly. This was it. This was where he was going to tell her that he and Vivian were just friends with benefits, or they had an open relationship, or some other thing that was going to make this a deal breaker for her. She couldn't get involved with someone who was already involved with someone else, no matter how they defined it.

He reached out and took one of her hands in his. She wanted to pull away, but his gentleness combined with the roughness of his calloused hands send a shiver of desire down her spine, and she couldn't bring herself to reject him. Not yet. She could at least hear what he had to say, couldn't she?

"Vivian is really vulnerable right now," he started.

She stiffened, prepared for some song and dance about how he'd just been trying to comfort her and one thing had led to another.

"Faith," he said, squeezing her hand, "it's nothing like what you're thinking right now."

She let out a huff of laughter. "Oh, and what am I thinking?"

"It's written all over your face. You think I'm involved with her. I'm not."

"Have you ever been?"

Hunter glanced away, focusing on the window behind her.

Her heart sank. "You were, weren't you? I guess I can't blame you. It happens a lot, people finding comfort with those they're closest to when grieving. How long ago did it end?"

"Over seven years ago," Hunter said, this time holding her gaze. "We dated for a short time before she got together with Craig. It lasted maybe a month, then it was over. The fight this morning was because Vivian seems to think we should pick back up where we left off all those years ago. She thinks it will be easier on Zoey. I keep telling her it isn't going to happen."

Faith sat up straight and blinked, trying to take in the new information. "You... used to date her?"

He nodded. "For a short period of time, years ago."

"And now you're just... watching over them for your friend?" she asked, wondering why he'd felt the need to bring his ex back to Keating Hollow. Didn't she have family somewhere?

"Sort of." He leaned forward, his hands clasped. "Craig asked me to be Zoey's godfather about a year after she was born. So in that sense, I am watching over Zoey. I'm just being a friend to Vivian. Her family's not real stable right now. She wanted to get out of Vegas, so when I mentioned I was planning on coming back here, she and Zoey came with me. That's it, Faith. Other than Vivian having unrealistic expectations, there's really nothing to be concerned about. I'm free to date who I want to. And I'm hoping like hell that you'll let me take you out on Friday night."

"Friday?" Gods, she wanted to say yes. There was no reason not to believe his explanation. She'd grown to trust him over the time he'd worked for her and hadn't known him to be anything other than honest. If he was lying, she'd find out soon enough. Secrets were impossible to keep in the small town of Keating Hollow. If he was seeing Vivian and dating Faith, the rumor mill would be working overtime.

"Yes, Friday. How about dinner? I could take you to the Cozy Cave, or we could go into Eureka if you prefer."

There was a nagging feeling in the back of her mind about Friday. She was forgetting something. Did she already have plans? The bridal shower wasn't until the following week. Was there a family dinner? Plans with Hanna? "I think I—oh!" She grimaced, remembering her date with Brian. "I already have plans on Friday."

He gave her a curious look. "A date?"

She nodded, not willing to start whatever this was with him on a lie. "With Jacob's friend Brian. But I'm free Saturday."

"Saturday it is then," he said, sounding amused. "I'll pick you up at seven. And this time, Faith, nothing is going to keep me away. Count on it."

"I will. But if you stand me up again… I'll start to take it personally." She grinned at him, her reservations about his relationship with Vivian settled. Yes, their situation was a little out of the ordinary, but she admired him for watching over his friend's family. It was just the sort of stand-up thing she'd expect out of him.

He stood and gently tugged her up off the desk. "Faith, one way or another, I'll be there." Hunter dipped his head and brushed his lips over hers again then murmured, "Make sure you tell your date he has competition."

CHAPTER 10

*H*unter bent down in front of his small cottage and gestured for Zoey to climb onto his back. "Come on. I'll give you a piggyback ride inside."

The little girl squealed and threw her arms around his neck.

He hooked his arms behind the backs of her knees and bounced her up and down as he made his way up the stairs of his porch. "How was school? Did you learn how to turn your classmates into toads?"

She giggled. "Noooo. That just happens in fairy tales."

"Oh. I see. Well then, did you kiss any and turn them into princes?" He unlocked the door and stepped through into the small foyer.

"Uncle Hunter," she said, sounding just like her mother when she was exasperated. "That's not real."

"Really? Huh. Okay then, what did you do today?" He set her down in one of the dining room chairs and went into the kitchen. After pulling steaks out of the refrigerator, he moved to the sink to wash his hands while Zoey rattled on about her new friend Daisy and the magic lesson of the day.

"We were supposed to turn a bowl of water to ice, but neither one of us could do it. Another kid in the class was able to do it once he stuck his finger in the bowl, but then no one could turn it back and they had to send him to the healer before he got frostbite."

Hunter raised his eyebrows. "They couldn't just melt the ice with warm water?"

She shook her head vigorously. "Nothing worked. His finger even started to turn blue."

"Ouch," Hunter said, salting the meat. "Did the healer manage to free him?"

"She didn't need to. Turns out he was holding the spell just so he could get out of a math quiz." Zoey rolled her eyes. "What a drama queen." She continued to chatter about the kids at school while he prepped dinner.

The sound of the front door opening caught his attention, and when he glanced up from the garlic he'd been mincing, he spotted Vivian leaning against the kitchen doorframe. Her eyes were full of love as she watched her daughter animatedly go on about her day. Vivian glanced over at him, and the two shared a smile. There was nothing better than seeing Zoey thriving in her new environment.

"Mommy!" Zoey called out when she spotted her mother. "You're home!"

Vivian took a step forward and opened her arms wide, and when Zoey threw herself into them, Vivian lifted her up and spun her around. "I missed you today, love."

"I missed you, too, Mommy." Zoey buried her head into Vivian's shoulder.

Emotion rolled through Hunter as he watched them. A

vague image of his own mother hugging him on a warm summer day tugged at his memory, and he smiled at them. This was what her life should be. Safe, stable, full of love. And as sideways as it seemed, this was also why he knew he and Vivian should never be together. Zoey deserved to have parents who loved each other with all their hearts, like Hunter's had before their accident.

The faded, dull pain stabbed at his heart as he remembered his parents. They'd been simple people who lived in the small town known as Keating Mountain. His dad had been the proprietor of the town tavern, and his mother had been a school teacher. But then one night a snow storm combined with a runaway logging truck had claimed their lives, and Hunter had lost them both, the only two people who'd ever really loved him.

"Hunter?" Vivian's voice cut through his memories.

"Huh?"

Vivian pointed behind him. "I think your steaks might be done."

"What?" He spun around and cursed. Smoke was filling the kitchen, and he hadn't even noticed. He reached over and turned the grill off. "Son of a... maybe we should go out to dinner?"

She chuckled. "Sure. Just let me change my clothes."

Zoey ran into the kitchen, eyed the charred steaks, and said, "Daddy always burned the meat, too. Did he teach you how to cook?"

A rumble of laughter escaped his lips as he reached down and picked her up. "No, baby girl. It was the other way around. I taught him everything I knew. That's probably why your mom banned him from the kitchen."

"So it's your fault?" Vivian asked, walking back into the

kitchen. She was dressed in a sweater, jeans, and leather boots. Her dark hair was swept up into a pony tail, and her cheeks were pink, making her look ten years younger. He hadn't seen her that relaxed in forever. Not since before they'd lost Craig.

He grinned at her. "Yes. I take full responsibility." Hunter carried Zoey over to her mother, draped an arm over her shoulders, and pulled her in for a sideways hug. "You look like you had a good day."

"I did. I went to practically every store in town trying to find clients. I even stopped by Faith Townsend's spa, but she was too busy to talk to me."

Hunter felt a twinge of guilt. He'd been the reason Vivian hadn't gotten to speak with Faith, but he wasn't sorry. It was a conversation they had to have, and it had resulted in the two of them finally giving their relationship a chance. He wouldn't take it back for anything.

"But that's okay. Her sister Abby hired me on a trial basis to see if I can help her grow the distribution of her lotions, soaps, and potions. If that works out, it's going to be really lucrative. Did you know she's built quite the mail order business already? You'd never know it judging by that little studio she works out of, but she's got quite the thriving business going."

"I knew she was doing okay, but I didn't know it was that successful. That's incredible. Congratulations. I'm sure you're going to shock her with how much product you're able to move." He gave her a sideways hug. "Well done, Vivian."

"Well done, Mommy!" Zoey parroted.

Vivian laughed. "Thank you, little miss. Now give your mommy a kiss."

Hunter handed the little girl off to her mother and for the first time since they'd lost Craig, he felt as if they were all going to be all right.

~

FAITH WALKED into her father's house with her mother's note tucked into her pocket and Xena the devil dog running in circles around her. As far as she knew, it had been twenty years since her father had heard from his wife, and Faith didn't want to be the one to bring her back into his life if he didn't want anything to do with her. Whatever she did next about her mother, she wanted her father's approval.

"Dad?" she called as she entered the living room. The television was on, a John Wayne movie playing on the screen. There was a blue blanket piled up on the overstuffed couch and an empty coffee mug on the end table.

"Faith? Is that you?" he called from the hallway. "I'll be right out."

Xena shot down the hallway, barking and growling as if she was going after an intruder.

Faith let her go and headed into the kitchen to make hot cocoa, the real kind with melted chocolate and whole milk.

"Xena, you crazy dog," she heard her father say. "Sit. Sit down and be a good girl."

The barking stopped.

"Good girl," he said. "I knew you had it in you."

The barking started back up immediately, and a second later Xena shot back into the kitchen, zooming around Faith's feet.

"I see the puppy lessons are helping," Lin said with a chuckle. "At least she knows what *sit* means."

Faith sighed as Xena grabbed the rug in front of the kitchen sink and started dragging it out of the room. "She's a work in progress."

Lin reached down and saved the rug from the fluffy little brindled shih tzu. "She'll grow out of it."

"That's what we keep saying." Faith stirred the hot chocolate and bit down on her bottom lip, not sure where she should start.

"What is it, baby girl?" her father asked gently. "Something's wrong. I can tell by the wrinkle in your forehead."

Faith pressed two fingers just above her brow. "I don't have a wrinkle, do I?"

He just laughed and opened the oven. The scent of freshly baked snickerdoodle cookies filled the room. After piling some on a plate, he put them on the counter and handed Faith two mugs. "Pour me some, too, will you?"

"Of course." Faith filled the mugs and topped the liquid with a squirt of whipped cream from the can.

Lin took one look at the mugs and frowned. "Faith, what's wrong?"

He knew her so well. Tears filled her eyes. Instead of saying anything, she pulled the letter out of her pocket and handed it to him.

Her dad gave her a curious look and asked, "What's this?"

"It came in the mail this weekend." A single tear rolled down her face, but she managed to keep her voice steady. "I'm not sure what to do with it."

Lincoln Townsend focused on the letter, and Faith recognized the exact moment when he realized it was from his ex-wife. He sucked in a short breath and stiffened. It took a few beats for him to hand the letter back.

Faith smoothed the paper just for something to do while she waited for his response.

Lin focused on his hot chocolate, brought the mug up to his lips, but then put it down without taking a sip. Finally, he turned to her and said, "What are you going to do?"

She gave him a sad smile. "I was hoping you'd tell me."

Lin reached out and put his aging hand over his daughter's and squeezed gently. "Baby girl, I can't make that decision for you. You know that. You should do whatever it is your heart tells you to do."

She turned to him, her tears dry now. "It's telling me to listen to *your* heart, Dad. I don't want to invite her back into our lives if it's going to hurt you."

Emotion flickered through his deep blue-gray eyes, and Faith was sure she saw moisture there. But he blinked, and his eyes cleared. "My relationship with her was over a long time ago, and I like to think I've healed enough that if she wants to try to forge a relationship with you girls that I'll survive it just fine."

Faith nodded, appreciating his willingness to put his feelings aside for his girls. "Thanks, Dad. That's big of you."

They were both silent, and Faith wondered if she even wanted to see her mother. What kind of person just up and left her family one day and never came back? Add in the fact that she hadn't wanted Faith to tell her sisters, and it just left a bad ache in her stomach. "I need to tell Abby, Noel, and Yvette, don't I?"

"Yes," Lin said without hesitation. "They deserve to know she's made contact with you."

Faith sighed and put her head down on the counter.

Lin caressed her hair and said, "It's okay, Faith. You don't have to meet with her if you don't want to."

"That's what Hanna said," Faith mumbled.

"You told her already?"

Faith lifted her head. "Yeah. I needed someone to talk to and she... well, she's my person."

Lin gave her a gentle smile. "Of course she is, honey. I just think you need to tell your sisters sooner rather than later. If they find out from someone else… well, Noel won't take it well."

"She won't take it well anyway," Faith said, but she was already pulling her phone out and starting a group text to them.

Are you guys busy? Can you come to Dad's? It's important.

Noel immediately texted back asking if their dad was okay. Lincoln Townsend had been diagnosed with cancer just over a year ago. He'd been going through treatments, and as of the last appointment his scans had been clean. But he was still weak from the chemotherapy, and the doctors said his immune system would be vulnerable for a while yet.

She bit her bottom lip and texted back: *It's not about Dad. It's about Mom.*

The texts from her sisters came in rapidly, each of them asking what about Mom and demanding answers.

Instead of answering, Faith texted back: *We'll talk about it when you get here. Dad and I have cookies and hot chocolate.*

Then she turned her phone off. She wasn't doing this over the phone.

"Come on, baby girl." Lin slid off his chair and kissed her on the top of her head. "Let's take these cookies to the couch and finish watching that John Wayne movie."

Faith chuckled. Her father never changed, and that was just the way she liked it. "Xena, come on, girl. Time to snuggle."

The young pup zoomed out of the kitchen and jumped up on the couch, commandeering her father's blanket. After using her paws to get it into just the right bunched up bundle, she circled three times and laid right in the middle of her nest.

Faith shook her head at the dog's silliness.

"Someone certainly knows how to get comfortable," Lin said, sitting right next to the puppy. Faith sat on the other side of her, tucked her feet underneath her, and dug into the plate of cookies her father had put on the coffee table.

Lin eyed the plate. "They better hurry up or there's only going to be crumbs left."

Faith shrugged. "It's not my fault they're taking their sweet time."

He laughed and turned the volume up on the television.

CHAPTER 11

"No. I don't think you should call her," Noel said as she paced back and forth in Lincoln's living room.

A fire was roaring in the fireplace, taking the chill off the November night air, but it didn't do anything to warm Faith. Her insides were ice cold and had been since the moment Noel had stalked into the house.

"She's trying to manipulate Faith, the youngest one. The one who remembers the least of what happened. No. It doesn't matter what she has to say," Noel raged.

"Noel," Abby said softly. "I know you're angry but—"

"You're damned right, I'm angry, and you should be too, Abby. She left on your birthday. She didn't even remember!"

Tears filled Abby's eyes and she looked away.

Yvette, who'd been silent up until that point, stood. "I think Faith needs to decide for herself."

"Vette!" Noel glared at her. "This is a family decision. And I say we don't do anything unless we all agree."

Yvette shook her head. "You know that's not going to work.

How would you feel if Mom had written you a letter and we told you it wasn't okay to answer her?"

"I'd soak the damn letter in vodka and then torch it," Noel said, her voice flat and void of heat.

Faith was sure she would have, too. She wondered if her mother knew that about her second oldest daughter? It was hard to imagine she did, but Noel had always been the one with a short fuse. She also held a grudge, and the biggest one Noel was holding onto sat squarely on Gabrielle Townsend's shoulders. Not that Faith could blame her. She was angry, too. More angry than she'd even realized. But now that Noel was letting it all out, Faith recognized the simmering resentment that had been building in her own gut.

"I'd call her," Yvette said, holding her hand up to stave off Noel's objections. "I want to know what she has to say for herself. I want to know what was so terrible about her life here that she just up and left us. All of us."

Abby reached out and grabbed Yvette's hand, lending her silent moral support.

"Does it matter why?" Noel asked as she flopped down into one of Lin's oversize chairs.

"Some of us need answers even if they aren't ones we want to hear," Abby said. "You know, closure."

"Closure is overrated," Noel said and rested the back of her hand over her eyes.

"No, it isn't," Yvette said quietly and glanced over at their father who was standing near the hearth saying nothing. "What do you think, Dad?"

He shrugged and shook his head. "She didn't write to me."

"He doesn't want to hear from her," Noel barked. "Trust me. She left him with four little girls. What more does he need to know?"

Faith watched Noel through narrowed eyes and, not for the

first time, thought her sister might be the most damaged of all of them. First their mother had walked out on them and hadn't come back, and then her first husband had done the same. Xavier, her ex-husband, had walked back into their lives a year ago. It turned out that he hadn't actually wanted to leave her and Daisy, but that didn't change the fact that she suffered from some serious abandonment issues.

"What if we find out she didn't want to leave?" Faith asked. "Would you want to know that?"

Noel scowled at her. "Like Xavier you mean?"

Faith nodded.

"I'll remind you that Xavier left of his own free will because he couldn't be honest with us. It was only later when he was drugged that his memory was altered. I don't for a second believe that Mom didn't have a choice, and honestly, since having Daisy, it's not anything I can understand or forgive her for. I vote no; don't contact her. And that's all I have to say about this."

"Abby?" Yvette asked. "Where do you fall?"

Tears stood in Abby's eyes as she turned to Faith. "I'd call her. Whatever her reasons, good or bad, I want to know. I want to put this to rest."

"One vote to call, one vote to ignore," Faith said. "Yvette? What do you think?"

Yvette hung her head. When she looked up, she met Noel's gaze. "I completely understand where you're coming from, Noel. The idea of walking out on Skye makes my stomach hurt, and I don't understand any woman who can just leave her children. But I have to admit, I want to hear what she has to say for herself. Not for her, but for me, so I can try to make some sort of sense of what she did. I still vote to call her."

"Two votes to call, one to ignore," Faith said under her breath.

Abby sat down next to Faith. "It looks like the decision is entirely yours, little sis. Whatever you want to do, we're behind you. Right, Vette? Noel?"

"Of course we are," Yvette said, taking a seat on the other side of Faith.

The three of them turned their attention to Noel, all of them staring her down.

She peeked at them from behind her hand and groaned. "You don't need my approval."

"Yes, we do," the other three said in unison.

Yvette smiled at her. "You're one of us. We care about what you think, too."

"Ugh!" Noel stood. "Fine. Call her. But tell her not to get in touch with me. She won't like what I have to say." She shook her head and walked over to Lin. "Goodnight, Dad. I'm sorry you have to deal with this. I know how much it hurts."

Lin wrapped her in his arms and pressed a kiss to her temple. "I let that relationship go a long time ago, love. My only concern now is you girls. I don't want to see you hurt again."

She nodded and hugged him tighter. "Don't worry about me." Noel jerked her head toward her sisters. "It's those three saps you need to worry about."

He chuckled. "Don't I know it."

FAITH PACED HER OFFICE, her nerves making her stomach do acrobatics. She hadn't eaten anything except a Danish from Incantation Café, and the sugar had only fueled her anxiety. How was she going to just pick up the phone and call her mother? She didn't even know if she'd be able to get words out.

And what would she say anyway? *Hi, Mom. Thanks for finally acknowledging you have daughters?*

Why was she stressing so hard? She really didn't have to say anything, did she? Her mother was the one who'd initiated contact. Faith could call her and just see what she had to say, right? That's what she knew she should do, but she couldn't. Not by herself anyway. She picked up the phone, but instead of calling her mother, she called Abby.

"Faith?" her sister said after the first ring. "Are you okay? Did you talk to her?"

"No. Are you busy?" Faith asked, trying to ignore the nausea terrorizing her gut.

"Not too busy for you. What do you need?"

"Can you come over and just... I don't know. Hold my hand through this? I thought I could do this on my own, but I'm so nervous I'm ready to vomit."

"Way to sell it, little sis," Abby gently teased. "Just what I wanted to do today—hold your hair back while you talk to the mother who ditched us."

Faith knew she'd meant for the words to be lighthearted, but they'd ended up coming out flat with a tinge of resentment.

"I'm sorry, Faith," Abby said quickly. "That didn't come out the way I intended. I'll be right over. Need me to bring anything? Chocolate? Wine? A voodoo doll?"

Tears stung Faith's eyes even as she laughed. "Just you. We can walk over to the brewery after."

"I'm on my way."

They ended the call, and Faith slumped down in her chair. She put her head down on her desk and tried to think of nothing other than the holiday Chocolate Stout she knew was on tap at the Townsend brewery. She didn't have any scheduled appointments that afternoon. If she wanted to drown herself in beer, she was free to do so.

There was a knock on the door, followed by Lena's nervous voice. "Faith? There's someone asking for you."

Of course there was. Being a business owner meant there was no time for self-indulgent pity parties. "Coming." She opened the door to find her receptionist standing there wringing her hands. "What is it, Lena?"

"Are you... um, making staffing changes?" Lena asked.

"Huh?" Faith stared at her in confusion. "No. What made you ask that?"

"So you aren't hiring?"

Faith frowned. "Not officially. We will need another therapist if business keeps growing, but other than that, I hadn't planned on it. Not yet."

Lena let out a long, relieved breath and smiled at Faith. "Good. I dunno what's going on, but the woman waiting for you in the reception room is going on and on about how she's going to transform this place and by the time she's done, you'll be kissing her feet in gratitude. I thought maybe you were hiring a new front-end manager or something."

That was the job Faith had promised Lena once they were big enough to warrant a full staff. "Definitely not." She gave Lena a reassuring smile. "I'm not letting you get out of our agreement that easily. I meant it when I said that was your job as soon as this place is up to speed."

"Thanks," Lena said, relief flashing in her dark eyes. "She just seemed so sure of herself, I guess it made me paranoid."

Faith slipped her arm through Lena's and said, "Come on. Let's go see what this is all about."

"Her name is Vivian," Lena said. "She came by the other day, remember? But you were uh... too busy with Hunter to meet with her.

"Vivian?" *The Vivian? Hunter's Vivian?*

"Yeah, she recently moved here from Las Vegas, I think she said."

Oh gods. It *was* Hunter's Vivian. What was she doing at the spa? Faith was dying of curiosity as she strode through the door to the reception area.

Vivian was dressed in chic black pants, stylish leather boots, and a flowy silk blouse that hung off one shoulder. Her sleek dark hair had been straightened, making her look like a runway model.

Jeez, she's gorgeous, Faith thought, and she felt a rush of jealousy as she walked over to the woman, her hand out in greeting. "Vivian, hi. What a surprise to see you again."

Vivian took Faith's hand in both of hers and said, "Your spa is gorgeous. Congratulations. I understand you just opened this summer."

Faith dropped Vivian's hand and nodded. "We did. It's been a challenge but rewarding nonetheless."

"No doubt." She glanced around and focused on the hand-carved pentacle that hung over the gas fireplace. "I can see touches of Hunter all over the place. He drew that piece for the artist to replicate, didn't he?"

Faith's mouth dropped open in surprise. It was a representation of the one that hung in the Townsend household, and Hunter had sketched it out for the artist who'd brought it to life. "Yes, he did. How did you know that?"

Her eyes glinted as she leaned in and whispered, "It's the tree right in the middle. He's drawn it before. I think it's a replica of a tree that was in Hunter's backyard as a kid. He and Craig built a treehouse and then spent much of their adolescent years using it as a hideout from the parental figures."

Faith stared at it and felt a rush of humble gratitude. It was the same tree that Hunter had used when he'd helped her with her store logo. It made her feel closer to him, special in some way. "Wow, I had no idea."

"It's such a Hunter thing to do," Vivian said with a quiet smile. Then she straightened her shoulders and transformed into a brighter, more animated version of herself as she picked up a bottle of Abby's handmade lotion and nodded her approval. "Great products on the shelf. Did your sister tell you I'm a sales rep for her now?"

"You are?" Faith asked, surprised. "When did that happen?"

"It's only been twenty-four hours, and I've already secured her a new account in Eureka."

"Wow, impressive," Faith said, wondering where this was going.

She didn't have to wait long to find out. Vivian walked over to the front desk, leaned one elbow on the counter, and said, "If you give me a chance, I can do the same for you."

Faith frowned. "But we don't sell products. Not our own products anyway. We sell services."

"Exactly." Vivian glanced around. "This place is gorgeous and high-end, but it looks like you could use some more foot traffic."

Being that it was the middle of the week during that time between Thanksgiving and Christmas, tourism was down in Keating Hollow, which meant the spa was quiet. They'd had a few clients come through in the morning, but that afternoon the place was a ghost town. And Faith had to admit to herself that if December didn't pick up she was going to have a hard time paying some bills come January.

"We are definitely trying to find ways to build our local clientele," Faith said.

"Great." Vivian beamed at her. "That's where I come in. If you're willing, I'd like to see what I can do about bringing you clients from Eureka and the other surrounding towns, regulars as well as tourists. Ones that don't necessarily get to Keating Hollow all the time and either don't know you're here or just haven't tried you out yet. I'd work on commission of course, but it would be a win-win for you since you only pay if I deliver."

Faith had been fully prepared to turn Vivian down for whatever job she'd been proposing. There just wasn't room in the budget. But with a commission-based position, she found herself unable to say no. There was no denying that they needed traffic in the spa to keep it open. Faith would be a fool to turn her down.

"How would we know the clients booking with us were a direct result of your marketing efforts?" Faith asked.

"Is that a yes?" Vivian asked, her grin widening.

"I think so. We'll need to work out some details, like your commission terms and how to make sure you get credit, but at first glance, it sounds like it's worth a shot."

"Excellent!" Vivian clapped her hands together. "Should we go into your office and work out the details?"

"Absolutely." Faith opened the door to the back rooms for Vivian and turned to Lena. "Abby's on her way. Just send her back when she gets here."

"No problem, boss," Lena said, sliding back behind the reception desk. "Hey, sales reps don't turn into front-end managers, do they?"

Faith barked out a laugh. "Not at A Touch of Magic, they don't. Don't worry. With any luck, now that we have Vivian on board, you'll be moving up sooner than you think."

CHAPTER 12

*I*t didn't take any time at all to hammer out a contract, and just as Vivian was leaving the office, Abby showed up with two steaming mocha lattes from Incantation Café.

"Here," Abby said, handing her the cup. "Drink this first. It will help."

"Abby, I don't think caffeine is going to help calm me down," Faith said, waving goodbye to Vivian as she took off down the street.

"No, but the brandy will." Abby winked and nodded toward Vivian. "Did she treat herself to a massage?"

Faith shook her head. "Nope. She's going to be a sales rep for us and find us clients while she's out hawking your wares."

"Really? That's fantastic." Abby's eyes lit up. "She already landed me an impressive account. I think you're really going to like her."

Faith already did. She appreciated Vivian's drive for building her sales business and loved that she was outgoing, a trait Faith felt she herself lacked. The only thing that made her slightly uncomfortable was the way Vivian talked about Hunter. There was admiration and wistfulness in her tone that made Faith sure Vivian had feelings for him. It could be really awkward to date Hunter and work with the woman who might be in love with him.

"Yeah, she seems great," Faith said and took a long swig of the spiked mocha. The liquid warmed her all the way to her toes. She held up the cup in a mock salute. "This was inspired."

"You're welcome," Abby said, taking a seat in front of the desk. "Okay. Do it. Just rip the Band Aid off. Call her and see what she wants."

Faith groaned, wishing she'd just tossed the letter without telling anyone. Then she wouldn't have to deal with this. But she knew deep down she would've regretted that decision. She took another sip of her mocha and tapped in her mother's number. She'd spent so much time staring at the letter she'd memorized it.

The phone started to ring, and panic welled up in Faith's chest. Her heart hammered against her ribcage, and if Abby hadn't been there squeezing her hand, she was sure she'd have thrown the phone across the room. Why was she doing this again?

"Hello?" The voice on the other end of the connection was both familiar and foreign. It had been so long since Faith had heard her soft, tinkling voice she was almost sure she'd imagined it. "Hello?" she said again, this time with a faint rasp.

"Mom?" Faith squeaked out. "Is that you?"

Silence.

Faith stared at Abby, barely able to breathe. Maybe her mother had changed her mind and didn't want to hear from her. Had she sent the letter in a moment of weakness? Did she want—

"Faith?" Gabrielle asked in the faintest whisper. "Faith, baby, is that really you?"

"Yes, Mom. It's me. I got your letter." She didn't know what else to say.

"Oh, goddess." There were tears in Gabby's voice, followed by a tiny sob. "You called. I can't believe you called. Thank you."

"You're welcome?" she said, making the words sound more like a question.

Her mother continued to sob quietly while Faith pointed at the phone and mouthed to Abby, *She's crying.*

"Good. She should be," Abby said with more venom than Faith knew she was capable of.

"Is someone there with you, sweetheart?" Gabrielle asked.

"Yes. Abby is here." She didn't explain why. As far as she was concerned, their mother didn't deserve an explanation.

"Oh. I see." The tears in her voice were gone, but Faith heard her suck in a fortifying breath. "Do Yvette and Noel know I wrote you, too?"

"Yes."

More silence.

All of Faith's nervousness fled as anger took over. She clutched the phone so tight she was surprised she didn't crack the case. Then she blurted, "What do you want from me? Why did you write to me now and not to my sisters?"

"Nothing... I—"

"You must want something. Otherwise you would've just stayed away." Faith pushed off the desk and started pacing her office. "It's been over twenty years. What is it? Do you need money? Did you just wake up from a coma? Are you sick?"

Cancer. The word flashed in Faith's mind, and she clamped her mouth shut, not wanting to know the answer. They already had one parent battling the terrible disease.

"No, no. Nothing like that. I just... I want to see you," she said, her voice fading out as if the wind were carrying the sound away.

"Why?" It was an honest question. Faith had no idea what she could want now after all these years.

"Because I miss my girls," she said, the tears thick in her voice again. "I messed up, Faith. I messed up everything. I just want to see you... to see if there is any way you and your sisters can forgive me."

Tears sprang to Faith's eyes, not because her heart ached for the mother who'd abandoned them, but because it didn't. The sound of her tears wasn't moving at all. They didn't touch her heart. All she felt was numb.

"Let me talk to her," Abby said.

Faith nodded and told her mother, "I'm putting Abby on the phone."

"Abby," their mother said, the wistfulness unmistakable.

Faith scoffed and thrust the phone into Abby's hand. She needed air, needed to breathe. The office was too stifling. She had to get out of there.

"Mom?" she heard Abby say.

It was too much. If she didn't get out of there, she was going to lose it. Without saying a word, Faith tore from the room, slamming the door behind her. She headed outside, needing the cold air to keep her head from exploding.

The minute she burst from the door, the scream came ripping from her lungs, a scream she hadn't known she'd been holding in. The sound was gut-wrenching, even to her own ears. She bent over and let out twenty years of pain, heartbreak, and confusion.

When the scream finally faded away, she fell to her knees and sobbed.

"Faith?" The low, soothing male voice registered in her consciousness, but she was too far gone to acknowledge him.

She knew Hunter was behind her, one hand on her back, the other gently holding her hand.

"It's all right, Faith," he soothed. "Let it out."

The tears came fast and hard and her body was racked by sobs. "She... left us."

"Who left you?" He brushed her hair over her shoulder, his movements deliberate and careful.

"Our... mom. She left and... never came back." She turned and looked at him, her heart raw with pain and pure emotion. "She. Left. Us. Now..." Shaking her head, she squeezed her eyes shut and wanted to scream again. But she knew the only way she'd get through this was to say the words. Say them out loud. Let them go. "She didn't love us enough to stay. Now she wants to be forgiven, and I—I can't. I don't know how."

His eyes widened. "You heard from your mother?"

She nodded and leaned into him, needing to feel something other than pain.

Hunter's arms came around her, and he pulled her into his lap. Pressing a rough palm to her cheek, he stared her in the eyes and said, "You don't have to do anything you don't want to do. You know that, right?"

"Yes. Intellectually, I know that. But in here," she pointed to her chest, "my broken-hearted little girl wants her mother."

With his arms still wrapped tightly around her, he slowly rocked her back and forth as the tears streamed silently down her face. "Want to talk about what happened?"

"When?" She let out a sad bark of laughter. "Then or now?"

"Either. Neither. Whatever you want." He pressed his lips to her head and gave her a soft kiss.

His tenderness, the way he was making her feel loved and

safe, calmed her, and the tears stopped. The contrast of his heat to the chill in the air suddenly made her feel alive and hyperaware of him and the fact she wanted him to touch her everywhere.

Faith cleared her throat, gently pushed away from him, and got to her feet. Her face started to heat with embarrassment, and she stared past him as she said, "I'm sorry, Hunter. I shouldn't have screamed like that." She let out a nervous laugh. "It's a good thing we didn't have any clients, right?"

He stood, too, and studied her with a strange look on his face. "Faith, what happened?"

She sighed, resigned to the fact that he needed some sort of explanation. He wouldn't just let her stroll back into the spa as if nothing had happened. She wouldn't if she'd witnessed him having a break down. "My mom, whom I haven't seen or heard from in twenty years or so, sent me a letter and wanted me to contact her. After talking to my dad and my sisters, I decided to call her today. And when she said all she wanted was forgiveness, I couldn't take it. I basically lost it. Major meltdown."

"That's a lot to deal with, your mother disappearing at such a young age," he said, shoving his hands in his pockets. "What did you say?"

"Nothing. I handed the phone to Abby and came out here to... I don't know, purge, I guess."

"Nothing wrong with that," he said. When she didn't respond, he added, "It's not the same, but I lost my mom, too. I was eight."

"She left?" Faith asked, relieved to be talking about someone else's experience. She didn't know how to process her feelings about her mom; she just knew there had been a storm brewing inside of her, and she had to get it out.

"She died… along with my dad. There was snowstorm and a big rig."

"I'm so sorry," she said, meaning it. "That must've been devastating." While her mother had just disappeared on them, they'd at least had their dad, who they all swore was the best dad who ever lived. Without him, it was hard to imagine where they'd be now.

"It was." He gently tugged her across the patio and pulled her down to sit on a bench—a bench that hadn't been there before.

She glanced around, finally taking in her surroundings. The patio had been laid with large, warm beige tiles, while the fire pit had been constructed of red and orange tiles. He'd also installed a matching curved bench off to the left from where they were now. The design was stunning. The colors fit in perfectly with the redwoods lining the property and were eye-catching all on their own. "Hunter," she said in a hushed tone. "This is gorgeous. I can't believe you got this much done already."

His eyes glinted in the late afternoon light as he gave her a pleased smile. "You like it then?"

She got to her feet and inspected the area. Behind them, he'd started a rock wall that would likely be filled in with native plants as well as a waterfall off to one side. "I love this. It's so much more than I was expecting."

He joined her, taking one of her hands. "I was also going to install post lighting around the perimeter, as well as ground lights around the steps over there. I figured it should be just as tranquil in the evening as it is during the day."

A thread of peace wound its way through her as she took in her surroundings, seeing the completed picture in her mind. Her eyes misted, but this time from pure appreciation and gratitude instead of sadness. He was turning her space into the vision she'd spoken about months ago before he left for Las Vegas. "It's going to be so lovely. We'll be able to rent it out for events. Parties, weddings, anniversaries."

"As long as it isn't freezing out," he said and glanced up at the darkening sky.

"Is the fire witch cold?" she teased as she slipped into his arms, hugging him.

He chuckled. "Not when you're in my arms."

Warmth spread through her, and she lifted up onto her tiptoes, pressing her lips to his. "Thank you."

"For what?" He brushed his thumb over her cheekbone, gazing at her as if he never wanted to take his eyes off her.

"For being here with me. I don't know what it is, but your presence just settles me."

"You know what, Faith?" he said, his voice a little gruff.

"What?"

"You do the same for me." He dipped his head and kissed her, sending tingles all the way to her toes. When they finally parted, they were both smiling like teenagers as Hunter walked her back to her office.

When they got to her door, she paused, not sure if she was ready for what was waiting for her inside.

"Are you going to be okay?" he asked.

"I honestly don't know." She turned to him. "Can you believe that at five years old, I was the only one who didn't cry when we realized that my mother left?"

He raised both eyebrows. "You're kidding."

She shook her head. "I did earlier that day when I felt as if something was wrong, but then I had some sort of premonition that she wasn't coming back. And I don't know, maybe I couldn't deal with the trauma, so I just didn't think about her. It's like I just cut her out of my life and my memory. She left, and I pretended she didn't exist."

"Until now," he said.

"Until now. I had no idea just how angry I was. And to be honest, now I wish I hadn't called. I don't think I want to see her." She stared down at her feet, ashamed of herself. This was her mother she was talking about, and no matter what she'd done, didn't she deserve at least one chance to explain? Faith wasn't so sure.

"Faith, listen," Hunter said, pressing both hands to her cheeks as he stared at her intently. "I know it's not anywhere near the same since my mother left involuntarily, but I can tell you that I'd do just about anything to see and talk to her once more."

"You're right. It's not the same," Faith said, her tone matter-of-fact. "And I don't feel that way. Not today anyway."

"I understand," he said, nodding. "And I get it. Trust me, I get it. There are people in my life... well, let's just say I have relatives who have let me down, too, and talking to them isn't on my priority list. But let me just ask you this one thing... if this was your last chance to talk to her, would you take it, or would you be content with your decision?"

"Do you mean if she ghosted again, would it bother me?" She really didn't think so.

"Yes... and no. Just ask yourself, if something happened to her and you could never speak with her again, never get answers, never let her try to make amends, what would that feel like?"

She leaned against her door and crossed her arms over her chest. "You think I should meet her."

He pressed his lips into a thin line and shrugged one shoulder noncommittally. "I don't know if you should or not." He pulled her in close and pressed his hand over her heart. "I think you should try to do whatever it is that's going to keep your heart whole."

"Dammit," she whispered, blinking back tears. "How am I supposed to know what that is?"

He kissed her temple and said, "Just listen. You'll know."

Faith hugged him tightly and whispered, "Thanks."

CHAPTER 13

*F*aith found Abby sitting at her desk, staring at the phone in her hand. She didn't even look up when Faith entered the office and shut the door behind her. Her footsteps echoed on the hardwood floors, finally drawing Abby's attention.

Abby's red-rimmed eyes met Faith's, and she said, "That was a lot harder than I expected."

Faith leaned against her desk and placed a hand over her sister's. "You don't have to tell me. I just had a meltdown outside."

Abby's lips twitched into a tiny smile. "A meltdown? You? That doesn't sound like my little sister."

"I know. Poor Hunter. He had to put me back together."

"Hunter, huh?" Abby asked with sudden interest. "What's going on there?"

Faith could still feel his arms around her as she said, "We have a date on Saturday."

"Oh, oh, oh! You should see the look on your face. You're smitten." Abby grinned. "Way smitten."

"Maybe." But the thought of being alone with him on Saturday made her giddy.

"Wait, don't you have a date with Brian on Friday?" Abby asked, her brows drawn together in confusion. "Are you dating two guys now?"

"No. I'm not dating two guys." Though, technically she supposed she was. "I think 'dating' is overstating things."

"So you have a date on Friday with Brian and one on Saturday with Hunter. Damn, little sister." Abby's eyes glinted with mischief. "You're a player."

"Calm down. Weren't you the one making eyes at Clay while you were technically still with whatshisname from New Orleans?"

Abby laughed. "Maybe. But I sure wasn't dating both of them at the same time during the same weekend. I'm impressed, Faith. Seriously. You go months without a date, and now you have the two hottest guys in town vying for your attention. Well done, babe."

"Thanks. I think," Faith said, feeling anxious about her date with Brian. She liked him, but she already knew the person she really wanted to be with was Hunter. She grimaced. "I don't think I'm cut out for playing the field. I should probably cancel my date with Brian."

"So… you like Hunter that much?"

Faith nodded. "More than that much, I think."

Abby gave her a sympathetic nod. "I get it. Good luck there."

"Thanks," Faith said. They both turned their attention to the phone that was lying on the desk. Faith bit down on her bottom lip before asking, "What did she say?"

Abby gripped the chair arms as her expression turned sour. "She's sorry. Sorry for a lot, it appears. For leaving. For only writing to you. For asking you to keep her letter a secret." Abby scoffed. "She said she wanted to ease back into our lives one at a time and that she thought you might be the most amenable because you were always an easy child."

"Easy? Sure," Faith said, matching her sister's scoff. "She has some nerve. Did you tell her no one is interested in her apologies?"

"More or less." Abby sat back in the chair, looking defeated.

"What is it, Abs?"

She visibly swallowed and then forced out, "I told her she could come on Sunday."

"You... what? She's coming here on Sunday? Where?" Faith's heart started to hammer against her ribcage. What if she melted down again?

"I told her she could come to my house." Abby closed her eyes and leaned back in the chair. "I didn't know what else to say."

"Your house, Abs? What about Olive and Clay? Are you sure you want that?" Olive was Clay's daughter from his first marriage and Abby's stepdaughter. She had just turned ten, and introducing her to a grandmother that was likely to flee again didn't sound like a good idea.

"No, I'm not sure I want her in our house at all, but I couldn't think of anywhere else that wasn't public. I'll have Clay take Olive to his mom's." She opened her eyes, her expression pained. "Was that okay, Faith? I didn't know what to say. But one thing I know for sure is that when I finally came home, I was tired of running. And the only thing I wanted was to reconnect with my family. That's what she says she wants too, and if that's true..."

"Your situation wasn't even close to the same as Mom's, Abby," Faith said earnestly. "You left Keating Hollow, but you never left *us*. Never. I know you kept your distance for your own reasons, but we always knew where you were and how to reach you."

"I know. I just... We don't know her reasons for leaving, and Faith, I think I really *need* to know. For my own understanding about what happened, I need her to tell us why she left." Her phone went off, causing her to jump. She fished it out of her pocket and read a text. "I need to go pick up Olive from a friend's house."

"Okay," Faith said, running a hand through her long blond hair. "Thanks for coming. I guess I kind of dumped this on you."

Her sister wrapped her in her arms and held on tight. "That's what big sisters are here for." When Abby released her, she gave Faith a devilish smile. "Now, it's up to you to tell Noel and Yvette."

"What? No. I'll tell Yvette, but Noel's your job," Faith said, holding her hands up and walking backward.

Abby snorted. "Please. You're the only one who could tell Noel without her stabbing someone with the closest sharp object." She rushed across the room, her keys already in her hand. Just before she slipped out, she said, "I'd call Noel sooner rather than later. She'll need time to calm down." She blew Faith a kiss. "Love you."

The door closed behind Abby, and Faith took her seat, staring at her phone. Shaking her head, she picked it up, cursed Abby, and called Noel.

HUNTER'S MUSCLES ached with fatigue after his long week of working at Lin Townsend's farm and Faith's spa. His body was screaming for a shower, a decent meal, and a nice long nap, but he was getting close to finishing Faith's outdoor sanctuary and needed her opinion on lighting fixtures. Not to mention that he was dying to see her, to touch her, and to wrap her in his arms again.

It was late Friday afternoon, and darkness had fallen over the town of Keating Hollow. But the stars were shining bright, and he wondered if he could talk Faith into a stroll down by the river. His aching body be damned, all he really wanted to do was spend more time with her. He knocked on her office door and waited.

No answer.

He knocked again.

When he didn't hear anything inside, he turned the knob and poked his head in. The office was dark. She'd already left.

Disappointed, he flipped the light on and headed to her desk, intending to leave a note and the fixture samples so she'd see them in the morning. But as he rummaged around for a pen and a piece of paper, he spotted a couple of old, faded pictures lying on her desk—pictures of a woman he knew. The woman who'd raised him since he was nine-years-old.

He dropped the light fixtures on the desk and held the picture up to the light to get a better look. He stared at Gia, his uncle's long-term live-in girlfriend, the one he'd both loved and hated for nine years until he'd left his uncle's house and moved out on his own.

What was Faith doing with a picture of his pseudo-aunt? He picked up the second picture and swore. Gia was front and center, with four little girls huddled around her. One had dark hair, and the other three were blond. He flipped it over and spotted the note scrawled on the bottom. Gabrielle, Yvette, Noel, Abby, and Faith Townsend.

He dropped the picture and shook his head. Gia was Faith's mother? How was that possible? Why would Gia leave someone like Lincoln Townsend and four beautiful girls to live out in the middle of nowhere with Mason McCormick? But he suspected he already knew the answer. And he for sure didn't want her bringing her troubles back to Keating Hollow.

After scrawling a note to Faith about the light fixtures, he pulled out his phone, took a picture of the photo, and sent a text to Vivian to let her know he'd be gone until the morning. Then he headed straight for his truck. He had a long drive ahead of him.

CHAPTER 14

$\mathcal{T}$he small cabin sat back among the redwoods, one light shining in the front window. The broken-down, rusted-out roadster was still cluttering the gravel driveway, and an old water-stained leather couch sat in the front yard adjacent to an old wheel rim that had been turned into a fire pit. It didn't look like much had changed at the McCormick residence in the four years since he'd last visited.

He pulled up beside an old Ford Bronco and killed the engine. Just as he hopped down the cabin's front door swung open, and Gia appeared on the porch wrapped in a blanket.

"Who's there?" she called.

It was then he noticed she had a shotgun in her hand. He rolled his eyes, knowing the gun was likely empty and that she still hadn't learned to shoot it. Still, he hadn't seen her in four years, and anything was possible. "It's me, Hunter."

"Hunter? What are you doing here?" She stepped back into the house, holding the door open for him.

"I need to talk to you." He bounded up the steps, surprised to find that the rotting stair risers had been replaced with solid wood. He glanced around and noted the entire porch had been redone.

"It's kind of late, don't you think?" She turned and disappeared back into the cabin.

He followed, ignoring her statement, and found himself in a clean and tidy cabin with a new sofa and matching club chairs. The old Formica dining room set was gone, replaced by a hardwood table and matching chairs. He blinked, taking it all in, and asked, "Where did all this come from?"

"We bought it." She'd discarded the blanket and was leaning against the same old tiled counter, watching him through skeptical eyes.

The kitchen was the same with the exception of upgraded stainless steel appliances. "With what?"

"Mason got promoted at work." She pulled a single cigarette out of her sweater pocket and rolled it between her fingertips without lighting it.

"At the logging company?" Hunter studied her, looking for the telltale signs of chemical dependence. But even though her eyes were tired, they were clear, and she certainly seemed coherent.

"Yes. He was made foreman."

There wasn't any pride in her announcement, just a statement of fact. And not for the first time, Hunter wondered if she felt anything at all for his uncle. "And you? Are you still making your… potions?"

She shook her head. "That's over. I've been helping Kimmy cultivate the flowers in the greenhouse over at the nursery in town."

"No side hustle?" he asked, still skeptical, even though the property looked better than he'd ever seen it. So did she for that matter. Despite the obvious fatigue around her eyes, she had a pink glow that wasn't unlike Faith's, and clear, bright blue eyes.

"No side hustle," she said with a sigh. "Why does it matter to you? You made yourself really clear the last time we saw you that you weren't interested in our life here."

"Because, Gabrielle, you're about to insert yourself into the life of someone I care about, and I'm not going to let you unless I know you're clean." He saw the surprise flash in her eyes the moment he said her real name and pressed on. "Why didn't you tell me who you were?"

She stared at her sock-clad feet. "I left that woman behind. It didn't matter."

"It sure the hell mattered. You stood there after Craig's funeral, listening as I told Uncle Mason about the work I was doing for Faith Townsend, while I praised her sisters and her father for being the heart of Keating Hollow. And you said not one damned word about being her mother. Why?"

Gia bit down on her bottom lip, looking like an older replica of Faith, and shook her head. "I haven't been her mother for over twenty years."

"And yet you've contacted her and want to reclaim a place in her life," he said dryly. "Why, Gia? Why now? Do you have any idea what you did to that family? What you did to your four daughters?"

"Of course, I know what I did!" She pushed off the counter and stalked toward him. "Do you think I don't live every day with the guilt and pain of losing everything? I had a husband who adored me and four beautiful girls. And what did I end up with? This." She waved a hand around at the small, shabby house. Despite the new furnishings, it was still rundown and in need of some serious repairs. "And a partner who never loved me. All he wanted were the potions I made. And then you came along, the sweetest little boy who'd lost his mom and dad, and I thought you were my chance to make it up to the universe, to take care of you, shower you with all the love I'd denied my daughters. But you..." She shook her head violently. "You didn't want me. I didn't deserve to stand in for your mother. I failed. Over and over again, I failed. Now I'm clean, and I want to try to start over. Is that too much to ask? Is it, Hunter?"

Emotion rolled through him, coiling like a snake in the pit of his stomach. He remembered the day he'd come to live with them. It was burned in his memory and always right there when he was reminded of that fateful day eighteen years ago. His uncle had picked him up from the sitter and brought him to this cabin. Back then, there'd only been one bed. Gia had thrown a sleeping bag on the leather couch in the living room —the same one that was now out in the front yard—and told him to keep quiet. She had a migraine.

She hadn't said another word to him as she cooked up a potion in the kitchen. When it was done, she downed it and disappeared into the bedroom with his uncle. They didn't emerge for three days. There'd been no food. No comfort. No answers.

He'd been nine years old, orphaned, and his new guardians were drug addicts. For nine years he watched them try to get clean, relapse, and try to get clean again. There were moments of comfort along the way, when Gia was soft-spoken and loving. She'd taught him to cook, helped him with homework, and welcomed Craig as part of the family. Then they'd be back on the potion, claiming they needed it to get well again. During those phases, he'd spent most of his time at Craig's house. When he was home, he was left to deal with creditors, dealers, and the underbelly of society while his uncle and Gia passed time in oblivion.

"I don't know what to say to any of that, Gia. It's not like I didn't give you a chance," he said.

"Right. A chance," she said flatly.

He didn't challenge her. He'd been the grieving kid who needed adults to make him feel safe, but he'd never felt that, not even when they were trying to get clean. "So that's what you're hoping to get out of Faith?"

Her sharp bright eyes met his. "I'm not evil, Hunter."

"I never said you were."

"Yes, you did. You just didn't say it out loud." She put the cigarette to her lips, still unlit, and simulated taking a drag. "I'm going to go see my daughters. It's part of my recovery. I'd appreciate it if you'd just butt out."

"I don't think I can," he said. "Faith and I are... involved."

She narrowed her eyes and glared at him in the way only a fiercely protective mother could. "You have responsibilities to that woman, Hunter. You can't just abandon her and that child for Faith."

It galled him that Gia knew anything about his situation with Vivian and Zoey. If it were up to him, they'd have been left in the dark. But after's Craig's accident, Mason and Gia had jumped in the Bronco out front and driven all the way to Vegas to say their goodbyes. Mason had been friends with Craig's dad before his death, and he'd felt it was his duty to pay his respects. While they were there, Vivian told them her plans of moving up to Keating Hollow with Hunter, and it was obvious they'd gotten the wrong impression.

He wanted to turn around and storm out. Every instinct told him it was time to leave. But he couldn't. There were still things to say. "My relationship with Vivian is none of your concern. I'm here because Faith needs to know the truth, and I want to make sure it comes from you."

"Does she know I raised you?" Gia asked.

He snorted his derision. Raised him? She was delusional. He'd all but raised himself. If anyone deserved the credit, it was

Craig's mother, though she'd passed on when he was just fifteen. "No. I just found out tonight you are her mother. We haven't talked yet. Are you going to tell her, or am I?"

"I'll tell her," she said. "My daughters deserve to hear the truth from me."

He was momentarily speechless. Gia had never been one to take responsibility, instead preferring to blame everything on her 'migraines' or Mason or Hunter. Or anyone else within spitting distance for that matter. "When are you going to see her?"

"Sunday afternoon." Her voice trembled a little, and it was hard to not feel at least a small amount of pity for her.

He had his date with Faith on Saturday. He wasn't sure how he was going to get through the night without telling her he knew her mother, knew her better than Faith did. But he was willing to let Gia do this on her own terms, just as long as she was honest. "If you don't tell her everything on Sunday, I will. Like I said, we're... friends, and I won't keep anything from her."

She closed her eyes and nodded.

"Good." He started for the door, but before he strode out, he turned back around and said, "I don't appreciate being used, Gia. Make sure it doesn't happen again."

"What?" she asked as her head jerked up.

"Don't think I don't remember you asking me all those questions about Faith and her family. You should have told me then who you were. I'd have given you their numbers if you had."

"No, you wouldn't," she said with utter confidence. "You care about her too much."

"You have no idea how I feel about her."

"No?" Her eyes narrowed as she studied him. "I think I do, otherwise you wouldn't have driven all the way up here and landed on my doorstep at ten at night. You're half in love with her already."

He started to deny it but just clamped his mouth shut and left without saying a word. She was right. He was half in love with her and had been since before he'd left town that summer. He just hoped that whatever it was that was blooming between them would survive the storm that Gia was certain to bring when she blew into town.

CHAPTER 15

$\mathcal{F}$aith changed her clothes five times before she settled on a red sweater, black wool skirt, and knee-high lace-up boots. She spent extra time fixing her makeup and curling her hair, and still she was ready thirty minutes before Hunter was supposed to arrive.

She pressed a hand to her stomach, trying to calm her nerves, and headed into her kitchen to pour a glass of wine. Her phone buzzed with a text message, and she frowned, hoping that wasn't Hunter texting to cancel. She grabbed the phone and let out a sigh of relief. It was Brian.

Sorry it didn't work out yesterday. Maybe we can reschedule for some time this week.

Guilt washed over her, and she felt terrible. She'd tried to call him twice to cancel but kept missing him, and on the third try she'd finally left a message letting him know she couldn't make it. She just couldn't lead him on knowing that she really wanted to be with Hunter. Now though, she felt she owed him an explanation.

She texted back, *Coffee Tuesday after work?*

Make it dinner. I'll pick you up at 6.

She stared at the phone and shook her head. It looked like he was going to get that date after all. Not knowing how to get out of it without creating drama, she texted back, *6 it is.* Besides, she liked Brian, and there was nothing wrong with having dinner with a friend. She just needed to make sure he knew that upfront.

Her wineglass was half empty when her doorbell rang. Her insides turned to mush as she practically skipped to the door. When she opened it, she found Hunter leaning against the railing of her porch, a single red rose in his hand. She stepped outside and smiled up at him.

"You look… incredible," he said, slipping one arm around her waist and pulling her to him.

"So do you." She leaned in and kissed him, his pure male scent engulfing her.

"That was one hell of a hello," he said, his eyes glinting in the porch light.

"It's not every day a handsome man brings me a rose." She took the flower from him, grabbed him by the hand, and led him into her house. After placing the rose in a slim vase, she turned and tilted her head at him. "Wine? Or should we head for the restaurant?"

He glanced at the bottle on the counter and then back at her with a wistful expression on his face. "As much as I'd love to stay here and have you all to myself, I think we should probably head to the Cozy Cave." He pressed his hand to her cheek, stared into her eyes, and in a low, gravelly voice said, "Otherwise you're going to go to bed hungry."

His tone of voice made her skin tingly, and she was tempted to say the hell with dinner. Instead she gave him a wicked little grin and said, "I doubt that, but it would be a shame to miss out on the crab-stuffed trout the chef added to the specials menu."

"You already know the specials?" he asked with a chuckle.

She shrugged as she took him by the hand and led him to the door. "Katie, the chef, came into the spa for a massage this morning. I got the inside scoop."

Hunter pressed his hand to the small of Faith's back as they walked out to his truck. It was a small thing, but his touch and his attention as he opened her door for her made her feel special, as if she really mattered. And when he climbed into the truck after her, it was the most natural thing in the world when he grabbed her hand and held it all the way until they parked in front of the Cozy Cave.

Although it was obvious to Faith that their mutual attraction was off the charts, their dinner conversation turned out to be surprisingly easy too. Hunter amused her with stories about the client who had a pet blowup dinosaur and would move it around his house on a daily basis. He'd found it sitting on the toilet, lounging in the pool, once even poking out of the fireplace wearing a Santa hat. She spoke of her sisters and their new obsession with golf cart races, and she had him doubling over with laughter when she described how Xena, the eight-pound shih tzu had managed to destroy three power cords, half a dozen shoes, four dog beds, and Faith's favorite sweater.

"I swear, she's the devil dog. I've taken her to every puppy training class within fifty miles, and she's failed every one of them," Faith said, throwing her hands up in defeat.

"But you love her," Hunter said knowingly.

She sighed. "Definitely. When she isn't destroying everything in my house she is the *cutest* little thing ever. And a great snuggler."

"You're the cutest thing ever," he said, grinning.

She leaned one elbow on the table and rested her chin in her hand. "Go on."

He laughed, and when the waiter arrived he ordered coffee and the flourless chocolate cake.

"I'll have the same," Faith said.

He raised both eyebrows. "I'm impressed. You don't share dessert."

"Nope. After growing up with three sisters, a girl learns to get her own." She winked and took another sip of wine. "Did you have any siblings?"

"No. Just me."

When he didn't offer any more information about his childhood, she turned serious. "You said before you lost both of your parents when you were young. Do you mind if I ask where you ended up? With your grandparents?"

Hunter picked up the bottle of wine they'd ordered and filled both of their glasses. After taking a couple of swigs, he said, "No. I went to live with my uncle and his girlfriend." He paused and glanced away before he added, "They weren't the best caregivers."

Faith's heart ached for the little boy who'd not only lost his parents, but then was thrust into a less-than-nurturing environment. "I'm sorry. We don't have to talk about this if you don't want to."

"I don't," he said, frowning. "But it's probably better that you know my background and what you're getting into before we get too far."

"You want me to know what I'm in for?" she asked.

"Yeah, something like that. Are you up for it?"

She met his troubled gaze, nodded, and gave him an encouraging smile. "Yes. You already know mine, I should know yours."

"Okay." He reached out and curled his fingers around hers.

"From what I remember, I had model parents. They were loving and signed me up for all kinds of things from soccer to guitar lessons. They were mad for each other and their only son."

"You play the guitar?" she asked. "That's really sexy, you know that, right?"

He chuckled. "Sorry to disappoint you, but I haven't touched one since my ninth birthday."

"Damn, and here I was already planning on being the president of your fan club," she teased.

"There's still an opening," he said with a glint in his eye.

"I'll keep that in mind."

He turned serious again and squeezed her fingers. "When I went to live with Mason and Gia everything changed. I'll spare you the details, but they weren't good guardians. Both of them were addicts."

Faith sucked in a sharp breath, and her eyes widened. "You grew up with addicts?"

Nodding, he said, "It was pretty ugly, Faith, but at least I had Craig and his family."

"Your friend that just passed away?" she asked, trying to make sure she was keeping up.

"Yeah. He was my best friend. We did everything together, and I spent a lot of time over at his house. His mom was an angel and without her... well, I probably wouldn't have made it. But I did, and I moved out of my uncle's house the day I turned eighteen."

"Gods, Hunter. I'm so sorry. That just makes me want to wrap my arms around your younger self and keep him safe."

"You can still wrap your arms around me," he offered.

She laughed. "I bet."

The waiter arrived with their coffees and flourless cakes. Faith took two bites, closed her eyes, and moaned in pleasure.

"Keep that up, and I'm going to drag you out of here in two seconds flat," he warned.

"You wouldn't dare." She made a show of taking another bite of her cake while arranging her expression into one of pure ecstasy.

"Faith," he breathed.

She giggled.

"You're gorgeous, you know that?" he asked.

"So are you." Faith forked another bite of chocolate and added, "So is Vivian."

He put his fork down and leaned forward, his expression serious again. "I already told you there's nothing going on there. Do you believe me?"

She nodded. "Sure. But I also think she wants there to be more, and that makes me a little nervous since she lives with you and all."

"You're right, she does," he said, surprising her once again with his honesty about the situation. "I already told you Craig was my best friend since childhood. We were more like brothers. You have sisters, so I'm guessing you understand when I say I'd do anything for my brother, including taking care of his wife and daughter."

"What does that mean exactly, 'taking care of his wife and daughter?'"

Hunter drained the rest of his coffee and said, "You already know Zoey is my goddaughter."

"You mentioned it."

"I plan to do my best to fill Craig's shoes for the rest of her life."

"And Vivian?" Faith asked, already aware that she wanted more than Hunter was willing to give. "What happens when she doesn't get what she wants?"

Hunter grimaced. "Vivian will do what she's going to do.

She thinks she wants me to step in for Craig where she's concerned. Be her instant husband and father to Zoey. I'm more than willing when it comes to Zoey, but when it comes to me and her, I think it's just her grief talking. She'll get over that soon enough."

"That must be awkward considering you're sharing a house," Faith said, uneasy with the situation on everyone's behalf.

He stared her straight in the eye as he said, "I'm one hundred percent not interested in her. Is it going to be a problem between us if Vivian keeps hanging onto hope that I'll come around eventually?"

Faith's fingers tightened around her fork. It did bother her that another woman had her sights on him. But he'd done nothing to indicate she couldn't trust him, and her gut was telling her he was speaking his truth. "I won't lie, Hunter. It does bother me. She lives under your roof and now she's working with me. It's messy."

"Too messy for us to move forward?" he asked.

She waited a beat and then slowly shook her head. Nothing was going to keep her from pursuing whatever was going on between them. "No. It's not. Just don't disappoint me."

"I wouldn't dare." He lifted one of her hands and pressed a soft kiss to her knuckles. "Are you ready to get out of here?"

"Yes. But just one last thing." Grinning, she reached for his plate and shoveled the last of his cake in her mouth.

CHAPTER 16

$\mathcal{F}$aith couldn't help the silly grin on her face as she walked into her father's house the next morning. Her date with Hunter had been perfect. They'd spilled their secrets, laughed, and made out like rock stars. It had been a close call, but in the end, she hadn't invited him to stay the night. She'd wanted to. Damn, did the gods know she wanted to. But this relationship was intense, and she was afraid if they moved too fast they'd be destined to flame out in spectacular fashion.

Hunter had been just as reluctant to leave as she was to send him home. But he'd kissed her thoroughly, promised to call her the following night, and then left her with Xena at her feet, chewing on the laces of her boots.

"Dad!" Faith called, wandering through his house. "Where are you?"

She heard a faint sound coming from the master bedroom and assumed he was on his way out. The teapot on the stove started to whistle, and Faith moved into the kitchen to fix them both a cup of tea. Five minutes later, when her dad still hadn't shown his face, Faith took both of the tea mugs and moved to stand next to her father's partially open door.

"Dad? Your tea's ready."

"Faith?" His voice was faint and a little weak.

"Are you okay?"

"No," he said with a moan.

Faith didn't hesitate. She swept into the room and glanced around, her eyes frantically searching for him. "Dad, where are you?"

She thought she heard a grunt and checked the master bathroom. He was nowhere to be found. "Dad!"

"Faith." This time she caught where the sound was coming from and ran over to the other side of the bed, finding her father sprawled on the floor, his foot at an odd angle. The same foot he'd injured just about a year ago.

"Dad! Oh no, what happened?" She set the mugs on the nightstand and crouched down beside him.

"I think I fainted," he said, staring up at her, his face so white he almost looked gray.

"Holy broomsticks," she muttered and reached down to grab his arms, trying to help him sit up. But the moment her hands touched his skin, she jerked them back as if she'd been burned. Tears flooded her eyes, and without saying anything to her father, she dialed 911.

The dispatcher answered on the first ring. "911, what's your emergency?"

Her words were muffled through the silent sobs she was holding back. "It's my father. He's fainted, twisted or broken an ankle, and he's very sick. He's got cancer and, I suspect, pneumonia."

The dispatcher confirmed their address and said, "A unit is on their way. Do you need me to stay on the phone with you?"

"No thanks," Faith said. But as she ended the call, she was

already wishing she'd taken the dispatcher up on her offer. She pressed a hand to her dad's forehead, and he flinched. "Too cold?"

He gave her a tiny nod, and her heart started to feel like it was going to pound right out of her chest.

"I'll get you a blanket," she said, not knowing what else she could do. If she had Abby's talents, she'd be able to whip up a potion that would at least fortify him enough to sit up. But she didn't. All she could do was sense that there was something seriously wrong with him. Wrong enough that it would be devastating when the doctor told them the news.

The ambulance sirens filled the air, and Faith let out a breath she hadn't even known she'd been holding. Help was there. People who knew what to do for him.

She ran to the door, flung it open, and directed them to Lin's bedroom. "He thinks he fainted. His ankle is a mess, he has cancer, and I'm ninety-five percent positive he has pneumonia."

"Is that a guess or do you have magic?" one of the EMTs asked.

"Water witch. I can sense when there are viruses or bacterial infections in the body. His is a bad bacterial infection."

Just as she got the words out, Lin's body was racked with a series of coughs that made Faith's blood run cold. Her father was sick, really sick, and it scared her.

"Thanks," the EMT said and went to work on inserting an IV. Moments later they had Lincoln Townsend on a stretcher, rolling him into the truck. "Are you riding with us?" the EMT asked Faith.

She nodded, jumped into the ambulance, and dialed Noel. Her sister answered with a curt greeting, as if she'd been expecting her call. "Faith, I'm still not meeting with Mom. I have no interest in hearing anything she has to say. Besides, nothing you can say can get me off my couch today."

"Noel," Faith said with a tiny sob. "It's Dad. He's very sick. We're in an ambulance on the way to the hospital. Can you call Abby and Yvette and tell them to meet us there?"

All of Noel's righteous anger fled as she said, "Don't worry about a thing, Faith. I'm on it."

"Thanks," Faith whispered to keep from sobbing in front of her father.

"And Faith?" Noel said. "I'm on my way, baby girl."

FAITH PACED the sterile hallway of the hospital, her insides twisted in knots. She couldn't shake the feelings that had flooded into her the moment she'd touched her father's skin. His illness had presented itself to her in an array of troubling emotions. Dread, agitation, and unease had settled in her bones. And then guilt that she was powerless to do anything about it. She could help strains and pulled muscles but was useless when it came to infections.

"Faith?" Noel rushed toward her, her mouth set in a grim line. "What's happening?"

Grabbing hold of her sister, Faith hugged her, holding on tight for a long moment. "The hospital's healer is in with him now. I called the Whipples. Martin is on his way."

Martin Whipple had been Lin's primary healer for the past fifteen years. He'd take over care after the initial assessment. "And his oncologist?"

"They said they called her, but I haven't seen her yet."

Noel sucked in a deep breath and nodded. "Okay. Abby and Yvette are on their way." Then she added. "He needs to stop doing this. My heart can't take it." She was referring to the time their dad had passed out early in the year from dehydration. Only Faith knew this time it was much more serious.

Faith stared at the double doors, willing the healer to return. Waiting was killing her.

"Come on," Noel said, tugging Faith down the hall. "Let's go to the waiting room. I'll find out from the nurse how long it's going to be before we hear anything."

Faith was too numb to protest. Her dad, the one person who'd always supported her unconditionally, was very ill. So ill it scared her. Rocked her to her core. She'd been brave during the cancer treatments, believing that her dad was strong enough to beat the disease. He'd put on a brave face and had been a rock through it all the past year. But finding him passed out and sensing for the first time just how sick he actually was had made her contemplate the possibility that they might lose him.

Tears welled in her eyes, and her breath caught on a silent sob, making her entire body tremble with grief.

"Oh, Faith," Noel whispered and gently pulled her sister down on the stiff blue couch.

Faith sat next to her, her elbows on her knees and her face buried in her hands. "I'm sorry," she choked out. "I just... when I touched him..."

Noel didn't say anything when Faith couldn't get the rest of the words out. She didn't need to. All of her sisters understood Faith's gift, both its power and its limitations. Noel caressed her sister's back and whispered, "He's going to be okay. He has to."

"Why?" Faith asked as she peeked at her.

Noel pressed a palm to her abdomen. "He'll be really pissed if he misses out on meeting his next grandchild."

Faith's eyes widened as shock rendered her speechless. Her

gaze landed on her sister's still-flat stomach. Then her lips curved into a small smile. "I didn't know you and Drew were trying."

She let out a chuckle. "I wouldn't say trying exactly, but we weren't doing anything to prevent the possibility either."

A thread of joy started to work its way through all of Faith's worry and she wrapped an arm around her sister, bringing her in for a hug. "Good goddess, Noel." Faith's eyes misted with happy tears. "This is the best news. I'm so happy for you. Does Daisy know?"

She shook her head. "Not yet. We were going to wait until after the wedding, but I'm not going to wait to tell dad. It seems like the right time to spill the beans."

"Of course it is." Faith's heart felt lighter with her sister's news. She and Drew were already great parents to Noel's daughter from her first marriage. She was overjoyed they'd be adding to their little family. "She's going to be so excited. Almost as excited as I am to be an auntie again."

Noel gave her a quiet smile. "Your auntie card is filling up nicely, isn't it?"

"Your little one makes four. Maybe we'll get a boy this time." A dull ache formed in Faith's gut. She loved her three nieces and was truly happy for Noel, but she couldn't help but wonder when she'd get her turn to be a mother. She wasn't in a hurry, but she sure wished there was more than a vague hope on the horizon.

"I'm not sure we'd know what to do with a boy," Noel said with a laugh. "The X chromosome seems to be strong in our family."

She had that right, though two of Faith's nieces had made their way into her life via previous marriages. Both Olive and Skye were technically her step-nieces, but no one saw them that way. Once someone was accepted into the Townsend family, there was no going back.

"Noel! Faith!" Abby called to them with Yvette right behind her. "What happened?"

Faith filled them in, doing her best to hold back her tears. The dread she'd experienced the moment she'd touched her father was still pulsing inside her, and she was certain it wasn't going anywhere until she felt for herself that he was improving.

"Yvette Townsend?" a woman wearing a white medical coat called. She was carrying a clipboard in one hand and a pen in the other.

"Yes?" the oldest Townsend sister said, getting to her feet.

"Ms. Townsend." She held out her hand. "I'm Healer Ricci, and I have an update on your father."

"Oh, thank the goddess." Yvette waved to Faith, Noel, and Abby. "These are my sisters. We're anxious to hear what you have to say."

"Let's have a seat," she said with a kind smile.

Faith studied her, wondering if the smile was reassurance or sympathy. She couldn't tell one way or another. "How is he? Is it pneumonia?" Faith blurted.

She turned her brilliant green eyes on Faith. "He's stable. He was dehydrated and having trouble breathing. We've started a saline IV and have him on oxygen until his numbers come up. We've also got him on a powerful antibiotic to fight the infection."

"So it is pneumonia," Noel said, leaning forward in her chair.

"We don't know for sure just yet," the healer said. "It's certainly a strong possibility. We've sent a culture to the lab and will know in a few hours. Either way, the treatment is the same. Antibiotics, fluids, and plenty of rest."

"And what about the cancer?" Abby asked, pressing her hand to her throat. "Has it gotten worse? Is that what caused his infection?"

"His oncologist has ordered some tests," she said. "But there's no reason to think the cancer has anything to do with this. It's more likely that his immune system wasn't able to fight off the infection due to the cancer treatments."

"So it is the cancer's fault, indirectly at least," Noel said.

"It's a possibility." The healer rose. "But keep in mind people come down with bacterial infections every day and they beat them every day too. Right now, the only thing to do is wait."

"Is he awake? Can we see him?" Faith asked.

"He's probably resting, but as soon as the oncologist is finished, immediate family can go in and see him." She gave them a short nod, spun on her heel, and disappeared back down the hallway.

"I'm going to get coffee," Noel said.

"I'll go with you," Yvette said.

"Abby, Faith?" Noel asked.

Abby shook her head and sank back down into one of the chairs.

"Nothing for me." Faith walked to the nurse's desk. "Can you tell me when I can go in and see my dad?"

The nurse took some information and disappeared. When she returned a few moments later, she said, "You can go in now."

Faith signaled to Abby, and holding hands, the two made their way into their father's room.

Lincoln Townsend was hooked up to beeping machines and a couple of IVs, his eyes closed.

"He looks so small," Abby whispered. "Like he could just fade away."

The raw pain in her voice matched what Faith had been feeling since she'd found her father a few hours ago, and somehow that made her feel not as alone. "He's going to be fine," Faith insisted. "Look, his cheeks have color again."

Abby moved to the side of the bed and took Lin's hand in hers. Bending down, she kissed him on the cheek. "Hey, Daddy," she said softly. "You know if you wanted a vacation, we could've taken a trip to the beach instead."

Faith let out a little chuckle. Leave it to Abby to try to add some levity to the situation. She moved to the other side of Lin's bed but didn't take his hand. She wasn't quite ready for what she might find when she touched him. For now, it was enough that his color had returned.

"You know how I like to make a statement," Lin whispered, the words barely audible.

"Good one, Dad," Abby said, her voice soft. "You scared Faith half to death. You know that, right?"

"Faith?" he asked, sounding confused.

"I'm right here, Dad," Faith said.

He turned his head a few inches to the right and blinked up at her. "I'm sorry, sweetheart."

"You have nothing to be sorry about," she said, knowing he was talking about her finding him in his bedroom. "It's a good thing I was there, huh?"

His eyes closed, and she saw his fingers tighten around Abby's. His breathing became steady, indicating that he'd already fallen back to sleep. Faith caught her sister's gaze and noted the silent tears falling.

Abby wiped her face with the back of her hand and stood. "I need to call Clay. I'll be back."

Faith watched her sister leave then took her place next to her father. She stared at his hand, fear and anxiety making her hesitate. But that was the only way she was going to know if he was getting better, if the treatments were working. She said a silent prayer to the gods and reached for Lin's hand.

She wrapped her fingers around his and held her breath. The dread, agitation, and unease came flooding back with a vengeance. She stood there, her feet rooted to the floor, willing the emotions to bleed into her, praying that if she took them on then somehow her father wouldn't have to bear the brunt of his illness. It was a futile attempt. She didn't really believe her magic could ease his suffering, but she just felt that if she could shoulder the burden somehow, he'd have more strength to fight the infection.

Tears streamed down her cheeks unchecked as his pain rolled through her. She didn't know how long she stood there, holding on tightly with both hands. This couldn't be happening. They couldn't lose Lincoln Townsend, the patriarch of their family, a pillar of Keating Hollow, and the best man she'd ever known.

While he slept, she brought his hand up to her lips and kissed his knuckles. "I love you, Dad," she said, her voice halting with emotion. "Get better. We need you."

Then she hung her head and just let herself cry.

The door opened, and she heard faint footsteps behind her, but she didn't look up. She couldn't. All that mattered was holding on to her father and not letting go.

"Faith," Yvette said, placing her hands on Faith's shoulders. "Come on, baby. It's okay. You have to let go now."

"I can't," she said, shaking her head. "I have to bear this pain for him."

"Faith." Her sister's voice hitched. Then she tried again. "Healer Whipple is here. He's going to look Dad over. We need to step out for a minute or two."

Faith glanced up, and through her blurry vision, she spotted Martin.

He was giving her a kind smile as he reached over and patted her hand that was still clutching Lin's. "He knows you're here, Faith. He knows you're lending him your strength. It's enough for now."

Yvette gently tugged her back. "Come on, Faith. We got you some tea, and someone is waiting for you."

"I don't want to see anyone," Faith said, but she placed her dad's hand down on the bed and let Yvette lead her toward the door.

"Trust me, honey. I think you want to see this one."

Faith couldn't imagine who it might be, but she didn't even care. The only place she wanted to be was sitting beside her dad, waiting for him to grumble about being stuck in the hospital when he had work to do at the orchard. But when Yvette tugged her down the hall, she saw him standing there, waiting.

Her heart swelled with love, gratitude, and something that felt an awful lot like relief.

Hunter opened his arms, and she fell into him, holding on for dear life.

CHAPTER 17

*I*t hadn't taken long for word to spread around town that Lin Townsend had been rushed to the hospital. Hunter had stopped at Incantation Café for coffee, and before he even got in line to order, he overheard Rhys telling Hanna that Clay had called to give him the news.

Hunter turned around, jumped in his truck, and headed straight to the hospital. He'd been at Lin's the day before working on the old barn and knew he'd been feeling under the weather, but he'd been out in his golf cart, checking his orchard just like he did every day. Hunter heard him coughing and told him he'd do whatever needed to be done, but Lin had waved him off, indicating that he was fine. Hunter had believed him.

It was obvious now that Lin had been pushing himself way too hard, and Hunter was kicking himself for not noticing. The moment he saw Faith's tear-stained face, he felt as if he'd been gut-punched. Yvette was holding her by the shoulders, appearing to hold her together as she steered her down the corridor.

Then Faith lifted her head and saw him, and in the next instant, she was in his arms holding onto him with everything she had.

"Hey, there," he whispered, smoothing her hair with one hand. "He's going to be okay."

She didn't say anything, just tightened her hold.

Hunter stood there for a long time, holding her, being the steadying force that she needed in that moment. Eventually, she pulled away and glanced up at him. Her eyes were red but dry now.

"Thank you," she said, her voice a hoarse whisper.

"There's nothing to thank me for," he said, meaning it. There was nowhere else he wanted to be. He knew what it meant to lose a loved one and prayed she wouldn't have to experience such devastation anytime soon.

"You're too kind." She didn't let go, but she loosened her hold just enough so that she could glance around the waiting room. "Where did my sisters go?"

"Yvette and Noel are sitting with your dad. Abby is with Clay." He'd watched them move through the hospital while he held Faith. "You should probably get a bite to eat, rehydrate."

"I'm not hungry," she said, already eyeing her father's room.

"I'm sure you aren't, but you need to eat something." He gave her a supportive smile. "If you let me, I can save you from hospital food. Or if you continue to resist, it's likely one of your sisters will force the hospital's turkey special on you."

She made a face and shook her head. "Turkey special? Please tell me you made that up."

"Negative. It actually exists. But there's a deli across the street. You game?"

"Okay. Lead on."

"Good choice." He entwined his fingers in hers and they walked hand and hand out of the hospital. Besides Zoey,

Hunter couldn't remember ever feeling so protective of someone, and it occurred to him that even though they'd only been on one date, that if Faith would let him, he'd never leave her side. The thought should've scared him, but instead, he felt content and settled as if he'd just found the person he'd been searching for his entire life.

FAITH WASN'T sure what it was about Hunter, but the man just inherently made her feel better. She'd been drained and had certainly overdone it when she'd been letting the effects of her father's illness seep into her, but once she was in Hunter's arms, it was as if she just released all of that heartache and tension right out into the universe. And while she was still worried and anxious to see her father again, she knew she needed the break and the food he practically forced her to order.

"You need fuel, Faith," he said. "Especially if you're going to camp out at the hospital all day and night."

"What makes you think I'm going to stay at the hospital all night?" she asked and then took a bite of her crab salad sandwich.

He gave her a flat stare.

She couldn't help the small chuckle that escaped her lips. "Okay, you're right. I have no intention of going home until I know he's okay."

"That's what I thought." He shoved a fry in his mouth and offered her some.

"Thanks." She ate two fries and stopped. She still had more than half a sandwich left and a bag of chips. "I think I'm done."

He eyed her uneaten food but didn't comment. He just wrapped her sandwich up and placed it back in the paper bag.

"You can have it later instead of the turkey." Hunter started to get up from the table, but when she didn't move, he sat back down. "What is it?"

"Why did you come?" she asked, narrowing her eyes at him. It wasn't that she didn't want him there. She did. More than anything. And that was the problem. She wasn't used to leaning on any man other than her father. If he was only there out of some sort of obligation to her or Lin because he was working for them, she needed to know before she got in too deep.

"You can't tell?" he asked, gazing at her so intently she started to feel as if he was seeing straight into her soul.

"No," she said, fighting to keep from crossing her arms over her chest to feel less exposed.

He picked up her hand and kissed her palm. "Because, Faith, that's what people do when the ones they care about need support."

"You care about me?" she asked, not surprised, but wanting to hear him say the words again.

"I think you know the answer to that question, but just in case you don't, here it is… I'm falling for you, Faith. I could no sooner stay away from you while you're in pain than I could Zoey when her dad was fighting for his life. That's how much I care about you."

Tears threatened to burn her eyes again, but she blinked them back. She had shed enough tears for the day. "Thank you. It helps that you're here."

"Do you want to talk about it?"

She shrugged. "What's there to say? He's sick, and they keep saying they are doing everything they can, but I know the treatment isn't working, or at least not working yet. And I'm so angry that I can't do anything to help."

"Of course you're helping. Just having you here lends him strength."

She wondered briefly if that's what they'd told themselves the entire time they were waiting for Craig to wake up. But she kept the thought to herself and sighed. "I meant that my hands are useless. I can't help clear the infection the way I can help speed the healing of sore muscles."

"I see." He lifted her hand and traced a light finger over the lines of her palm. "Your hands are magic, Faith. The people of Keating Hollow are blessed to have you, but if you're upset with yourself because you can't heal your father, you're putting way too much pressure on yourself. Even the healers can't do what you're suggesting."

She knew he was right. They were pumping her father with antibiotic potions and energy boosters. No doubt they'd bring in healers with healing hands, but they wouldn't do that until he was stronger, when his body had the energy to help itself. "I know. I just... I can't stand to see him so sick. He's the lifeblood of our family, Hunter. If he..." She shook her head. "We can't lose him."

"You won't." His words were strong and sure, and they were like a balm on her aching heart. He stood, and she rose with him. "Let's go see how he's doing."

"Hunter?"

He reached over and grabbed the bag that contained her half-eaten sandwich. "Yeah?"

"I'm glad you're here." She leaned in and kissed him. His lips were warm and soft and exactly what she needed. When she pulled away, she smiled up at him. "And thanks for pretending I don't look like a hot mess."

"All I see is a gorgeous woman who's not afraid to show her emotions." He tugged her forward and said, "Let's go before the guy behind the counter tries to steal you from me."

She glanced back at the balding guy using one of the machines to slice cheese. He was staring right at her, interest sparking in his big eyes. She smiled up at him. "I think you could take him."

"Maybe, but there's no telling what kind of magic he's packin'."

She laughed and followed him out of the deli and back into the hospital.

It didn't take long to figure out something was seriously wrong. The minute they arrived in the waiting room, the tension was so thick Faith's skin actually started to itch. Yvette was standing near the window, staring out at the parking lot, while Abby was frantically texting on her phone. Noel was speaking to the nurse, her body trembling with what Faith thought must be anger.

"What's wrong?" Faith asked.

Abby looked up from her phone and stared pointedly at a woman sitting across the room. Her honey-blond hair had been curled, and it framed her familiar face.

Faith let out a small gasp and could've sworn she heard Hunter curse under his breath, but she was too focused on the woman staring back at her. "Mom?"

Gabrielle slowly pushed herself out of her chair. She was thin, maybe too thin, and although she'd obviously taken care to style her hair, her locks were in desperate need of a cut and color. But it was her eyes that haunted Faith. They were sad with a touch of weariness, the mark of a woman with a million regrets.

"She shouldn't be here," Noel snapped. "I can't believe she just showed up here like this after all these years." She turned to Gabrielle. "You're not welcome here."

"Noel, please," Abby said, pleading with their sister. "Now isn't the time."

"No, it isn't. Our dad is sick, and we don't have time to indulge her." Noel snapped her attention back to the nurse. "She's not to see Lincoln Townsend, do you understand? He doesn't want to have anything to do with her."

"You don't know that," Abby said.

"Noel's probably right," Yvette chimed in, finally turning to stare at their mother. "At the very least, we should wait until he's coherent to ask him."

"We won't let anyone in who isn't immediate family," the nurse said. "You don't have to worry about that."

"I'm his wife," Gabrielle said.

Everyone turned to stare at her. Faith couldn't believe she'd had the gall to claim some sort of marital privilege after all the years she'd been gone. And as she stood there staring at the woman she'd spent most of her life wishing would walk back into her life, Faith felt nothing. Not anger, not regret, and certainly not joy. She was indifferent, and that just made her sad.

"She's his ex-wife," Noel shot back. "Ex. Dad filed for abandonment over fifteen years ago. You don't get to just waltz back into his life, our lives, and act like nothing happened." She pointed to the exit. "You should go."

Gabrielle glanced around the room at her four daughters, and Faith had to avert her gaze. She couldn't handle her mother's haunted eyes. Not then. Not when all of her energy was focused on her father lying in a hospital room.

"I understand," Gabrielle said softly. "I didn't mean to intrude. I just..." She shook her head. "I hope Lin is all right." Then she ran out of the waiting room.

Abby let out a little sob, and in the next moment, she took off after her.

Faith, Yvette, and Noel stared after them in silence. Then Yvette let out a sigh and followed Abby.

"What about you?" Noel asked Faith. "Are you going to let her just waltz back into your life like nothing happened?"

Faith didn't appreciate her sister attacking her, but she understood where the anger was coming from and instantly forgave her. "No. I don't think so," Faith said. "I don't have it in me."

Noel closed her eyes and nodded. Then she turned to the nurse and said, "I'm sorry. We had no idea she was coming."

"It's all right, dear," the nurse said. "We've seen it all."

"Are you all right?" Hunter whispered in her ear.

She turned and pressed her hand to his chest. "As okay as I can be."

He stared down at her, seeming to search her face for any sort of emotional distress.

"I swear. I'm okay. I really don't have the emotional energy to deal with her right now. It was strange seeing her, but I just felt… nothing. I guess I purged everything the other day when I spoke to her."

He brushed a lock of hair out of her eyes. His touch was so tender, she wished he'd never stop. But then he dropped his hand and pulled back. "There's something I need to take care of. Are you going to be all right?"

"Sure," she said, frowning. "Don't tell me you're doing work at my dad's place or the spa, because—"

"It's not that," he said, cutting her off. "I just need to make a phone call. I'll be back."

Right. He probably needed to call Vivian. The thought bothered her. If there wasn't anything between them, why did he have to call and check in? She immediately felt ashamed. It probably had to do with Zoey. He'd already told her that he was stepping in to fill Craig's shoes. It only made sense he'd be communicating with Vivian. "Sure. Thanks for stopping by. Having you here really made a difference."

He gave her a strange look. "Were you under the impression I was leaving?"

"Well..."

He chuckled. "Faith, I'm glad I made a difference, but I'm not going anywhere yet. I just need to take care of something. I'll meet you back here, okay?"

"Okay." She gave him a sheepish smile. "Sorry. It's been a day."

"I know." He bent down, kissed her, and then strode off.

Faith sat down in one of the chairs, suddenly exhausted.

"That's a new development," Noel said, taking the seat next to her.

"Yeah." Faith said with a sigh. "We had our official first date last night."

Noel ran a knuckle over Faith's cheek. "Is that why you have whisker burn?"

Faith jerked back. "I don't have whisker burn!"

"You just keep telling yourself that, little sister," she said with a laugh. Then she turned and eyed her. "For the record, it looks good on you."

Faith rolled her eyes. "Stop. You're embarrassing me."

"That's what big sisters are for."

"Trust me, I know." As the youngest, Faith had taken the brunt of the sisterly teasing her entire life. But she'd also been blessed with three older siblings who'd stood up for her just as often. Faith glanced at the hallway leading to her dad's hospital room. "Have you been in to see him lately?"

"Just a few minutes before Gabrielle showed up. They gave him a sedative to help him sleep."

It didn't escape her notice that Noel was calling their mother by her first name. Noel wasn't even ready to talk to her, much less call her Mom. "Why the sedative? He was sleeping fine when we were in there earlier."

"Fever dreams were making him restless. Martin said that when the antibiotics start to kick in the dreams will stop."

Faith stood, intending to head back into his room, to just sit by him while he slept, but a giant yawn overtook her, and her eyes started to water. She glanced down at Noel. "I think I'm going for some coffee. Need some?"

Noel pressed two fingers to her temple and said, "Yes. Large. Black."

"Got it." Faith headed down the hospital hallway, looking for the cafeteria. Unsure of where to go, she made two wrong turns before she backtracked and ended up in a part of the hospital she didn't recognize. After consulting a map on the wall, she headed out the glass doors, intending to cross the campus, and came to a dead stop.

Off to the right, near a cluster of trees, she spotted her mother and Hunter. His entire body was tense, and his hands were curled into fists. There was no question he was angry. But about what? Gabrielle intruding on her and her family? She started to move toward them but froze again when her mother raised her voice and pointed a finger at him.

"And what about you, Hunter?" she said, her voice carrying in the December air. "Have you been honest with her? Have you told Faith that I'm the one who raised you and you've known all along where I've been? And what about Zoey? Does she know who her real father is? Don't talk to me about honesty. We all have our secrets. When all of your skeletons are outed, then maybe you'll have room to lecture me. Until then, keep it to yourself."

A cold chill ran through Faith as she waited for Hunter to contradict her. To deny her accusations. But he didn't. Instead he said, "I'll tell her in my own good time."

I'll tell her in my own good time. The words rang in Faith's head. He hadn't denied anything. What she'd said was true.

Gabrielle had raised Hunter? Hadn't he said he'd lived with his uncle and his live-in girlfriend, Gia? *Gia* was a nickname for Gabrielle. And what about Zoey? Had her mother just implied that Zoey was really Hunter's, not Craig's?

She had, and Hunter hadn't denied any of it.

Everything he'd said had been a lie. Her entire body was numb as she calmly turned around and walked back into the hospital.

CHAPTER 18

*H*unter fumed silently as he walked around the hospital campus trying to work off some of his anger. He couldn't believe that Gia had just shown up at the hospital with no warning. He understood that she'd been invited to Keating Hollow to see her daughters, but that was before Lin had been rushed to the emergency room.

He didn't care how worried she was about Lin or her daughters. Today wasn't the day for her crap. And worse, when he'd found her talking with Abby and Yvette, she hadn't been truthful about where she'd been. He'd overheard her say something about Tucson, Arizona, making it sound as if she wasn't just a few hours' drive away. After Abby and Yvette made their way back inside, he'd taken Gia by the elbow and let her know in no uncertain terms that he wasn't going to allow her to lie to her family. If she was determined to reconnect, they deserved to know the truth about her.

That's when she'd thrown the only crap she could at him and accused him of lying to Faith. He hadn't. At least not about his relationship with Gia. Hadn't he just found out who she really was? He'd intended for Gia to tell Faith and her sisters about her past. But if she was going to lie, then he'd have no choice. He wasn't a man who kept secrets from those he cared about.

When it came to Zoey... well, Zoey didn't even know the truth yet. And until she did, Hunter wasn't going to be broadcasting the fact that he was her biological father. When the time was right, they'd tell her. Until then it wasn't anyone's business... including Gia's. The only reason she knew was because when she and Mason had come to Craig's funeral, they'd overheard Hunter and Vivian arguing about how to handle it.

The last person he would've told was Gia. If she managed to stay clean, she'd keep the knowledge to herself, but if she had a lapse and got back on the potions, there was no telling what she'd do or say.

Hunter walked the perimeter of the hospital a half dozen times before he finally headed back to the waiting room. He wanted to check on Faith and see if he could do anything for her. Make sure she was okay.

He found her standing near a window, staring out at the town of Eureka with a cup of coffee in her hand. Placing his palm on the small of her back, he whispered, "Hey. How's it going? You doing okay?"

She didn't even turn to look at him as she said, "Doing fine." Her tone was void of emotion as she asked, "Did you get your *errand* done?"

"Sure." He frowned. Was it his imagination, or was she angry at *him*? She seemed cold and distant. But even as the thought popped into his mind, he berated himself. Her father was seriously ill, and her long-lost mother had just walked back into her life at the worst possible moment. Of course she wasn't okay. Anyone could see that. Asking her to ease his fears was only making things worse. "Any change with your dad?"

She shook her head, still not looking at him. "None."

Her body was so tense that her muscles bunched as if she were waiting to strike at someone. Her mother, probably. Or even just the universe for inflicting cancer and life-threatening bacterial infections on her father.

"Try to relax a little, Faith," he said, placing his hands on her shoulders and kneading at the knots he found there.

Faith let out an audible sigh and stepped away from him, putting enough distance between them that he couldn't touch her without moving forward.

"Too hard?" he asked, referring to the amateur massage he'd just tried to give to a certified massage therapist.

"I think you should probably go, Hunter. I need to focus on my dad and my family right now."

"Oh, all right," he said, shoving his hands into his pockets. "I didn't mean to overstay my welcome."

She didn't respond.

Hunter wanted to reach out and envelop her in his arms, hold her, and make sure she felt loved, but the determined look in her eyes and her closed-off body language held him back. She clearly wasn't interested in being taken care of anymore. "Okay then. You'll call if there's anything I can do?"

"I won't call. There's nothing anyone can do but wait. Thanks for stopping by. That was thoughtful of you."

Something was seriously wrong, and he thought he knew exactly who he should blame for her abrupt personality change. Gia. She'd waltzed right in and stirred up a storm. The anger he'd contained before walking back into the hospital came roaring back, but he kept it buried. Faith already had enough of her own emotional baggage, she didn't need to deal with his as well.

"Even so," he insisted, "don't hesitate to call me if you need anything. Food, coffee, a ride, someone to talk to. I'm here for whatever you need."

"Thank you, Hunter. I appreciate that, but like I said, we'll be fine." She turned and walked back down the hallway, disappearing when she rounded a corner.

He glanced around at the other Townsend sisters. Noel was standing by herself, talking on the phone, while Abby and Yvette had their heads bent together debating what they should do about their mother. It appeared that both Noel and Faith had said they weren't interested in anything she had to say, but the other two wanted answers. Hunter knew he could fill them in on Gia's life, but he also knew that wasn't his place. Besides, if he was going to tell anyone, he'd tell Faith first, and she wasn't in any condition to hear why her mother had abandoned them when they'd needed her most.

With his head down and his heart heavy from not being able to do more, he left the hospital and headed home.

It was late afternoon when Hunter pulled his truck into his driveway right next to a silver Honda SUV. His small cottage was all lit up with light flooding out the windows, and Hunter groaned. Did Vivian have guests? She hadn't mentioned anything to him. He hadn't even known she'd met many people yet other than Abby and Faith.

Bone weary, he climbed out of his truck and reluctantly made his way inside. He'd expected to hear voices or laughter or anything to indicate there were people milling around his house, but he was greeted by silence. Not even the sound of Zoey's feet on the hardwood since she wasn't running to greet him like she usually did.

"Vivian?" he called out.

No response.

"Zoey?"

Still nothing. He hung his coat on the rack near the door and wondered if they'd taken a walk or were out with the owner of the silver SUV. Relief washed over him as he realized he must be alone. Good. All he wanted to do was grab a beer, a shower, and a sandwich—in that order—before sinking into his couch. But when he stepped into the kitchen, he spotted Vivian sitting at the table with her arms crossed over her chest.

"Whose car's outside?" he asked, glancing around.

"Mine. I bought it today. Used. I needed something reliable to get me to Eureka and back."

"Sounds like a plan."

Her eyes were fixed on him as she said, "Hunter, I think we should talk."

Dread and irritation had him clamping his mouth shut as he reached for a bottle of beer from the fridge. Without acknowledging her, he popped the top and took a long fortifying swig.

"Did you hear me?" she asked, a challenge in her tone.

He turned around and leaned against the counter. "I heard you. What is it we need to talk about?"

She eyed him and then his beer. "I think I could use one of those."

Hunter shrugged, grabbed another beer, opened it for her, and set it on the table in front of her.

After she took a long sip of her own, she glanced up at him and said, "I can't do this anymore."

"Do what exactly?" His insides turned into a mess of jumbled nerves, waiting to find out what she meant. Live in his house? Share Zoey with him? Stay in Keating Hollow? Every one of those scenarios made him uneasy. The thought of her taking Zoey away from him made him want to vomit.

"Pretend we're a family when we're not." She stared down at the table, nervously tracing the grain of the wood with her fingertips.

"We're family. We're Zoey's parents," he said, glancing around for his little girl. "Where *is* Zoey by the way?"

"She's with Daisy and Olive at Olive's grandmother's house. Clay is going to drop her off after he picks them all up later."

He nodded. "That's good. She's making friends quickly."

But Vivian shook her head. "No, Hunter. It isn't good. Not when I'm going to have to move her again."

"Move?" He put his beer down on the counter. "What do you mean move?"

"I can't do this. I thought I could, but after watching you take Faith out last night and then today…" She closed her eyes and shook her head slightly. "You spent all day with her at the hospital."

"So? Her dad, my employer, is very sick. I was just there to—"

"I know why you were there," she said, her tone heated. "I'm not an idiot, Hunter. Or maybe I am. Because I was the one stupid enough to think that once we got here, once we were sharing a house and raising Zoey together, that you'd see me as someone more than Craig's wife. That you'd start to see me as a woman again, one you might be able to share a life with. I don't want a pretend family, Hunter. I want it all. And I foolishly thought that could include you."

He stared at her, stunned. "But I… we talked about this, Vivian."

"No, you talked about it." She stood up, the wooden legs of the chair squeaking on the floor. "I listened and hoped you'd change your mind. But it's obvious to me now that you're completely into someone else. Of course you are." She let out a hollow laugh. "Why else would you shut down the possibility of us becoming something more so quickly?"

"We were only together for a month or so, Viv," he said, still trying to make sense of everything. "I don't understand how that translates to a 'life together.'"

"We have a child together!" she yelled, tears streaming down her cheeks. "I guess I foolishly thought it would be nice for her parents to be together. If I'd known back then that she was yours, I wouldn't have let you go so easily. You have to know that."

"Whoa, hold on just a second," he said, pulling out a chair and sitting down. He tugged her down into her chair and looked her straight in the eye. "You loved Craig. You guys were great together. Why would you say that?"

She slumped into the chair and wiped her tears with one hand. "I did love him. I loved him with everything I had."

"That's good, Viv. He loved you, too. Why would I have wanted to stand in the way of that?"

"It's not... Ugh! I just mean that I think parents should try to make it work. I was into you back then you know. Before Craig and I got together. If I'd known about Zoey, if I'd realized she was yours, I would have told you. And who knows what would've happened? You have to believe me, Hunter. I really had no idea."

He did believe her. They'd only found out that Hunter was Zoey's father after Craig needed a rare blood type for a transfusion after his accident. A type that made it impossible for him to be Zoey's father. Vivian had been just as shocked as he was. Craig died never knowing the truth. And for that, Hunter was grateful. Craig had loved Zoey with all his heart. If he'd found out later she belonged to Hunter, it would've gutted him.

Hunter had been in denial at first. Zoey was small when she was born, small enough that everyone believed she'd come early. But in reality, she'd been a couple weeks late, and a blood test had proved it. Between Craig's death, Hunter's promise to him to take care of his family, and the revelation that Zoey was Hunter's biological child, it had been enough to rock him to his core.

But in the end, he'd done the only thing he could do—packed up his child and her mother and brought them home. Abandoning them was out of the question. Not that he'd wanted to. He loved Zoey more than he could've ever imagined loving another person.

"I believe you," he said. "And I understand what you're saying, but I don't think a child is enough to keep two people together. Not when they don't love each other."

"I could've loved you." She lowered her voice and added, "I think I *did* love you."

Hunter's heart was in his throat. What was he supposed to say to this woman, the mother of his child, his best friend's widow? He hadn't loved her. He'd liked her and found her attractive, but he had known from the start that she wasn't the one. It was why their relationship had burned hot and flamed out fast. It was also why he hadn't cared in the least when Craig started dating her. He'd been happy for them.

Finally, he just said, "Where are you planning to go? And will I still get to see my daughter?"

"Eureka. Most of my work is done there anyway trying to find clients for Faith and accounts for Abby. I checked out the schools. There is one on the north end of town that would be perfect for Zoey. It's the sister school to the one here in town with the same curriculum."

Hunter hated the idea that he wouldn't see Zoey every day, that he couldn't tuck her in or read her stories, but what could he say? He couldn't pretend to love Vivian just so she'd stay. At least she wasn't going back to Las Vegas. "All right."

She sighed heavily. "You're not even going to try to stop me?"

He shook his head. "I can't make you stay if you don't want to be here. But I do want shared custody of my daughter."

"We're going to have to tell her," Vivian said.

"I know." They'd decided to hold off on breaking the news to Zoey. She'd just lost the father who'd raised her, and her whole life had been uprooted. They'd both decided it was better to wait, but the longer they waited, the harder it was going to be on all of them.

"I'm going to look for a place tomorrow," she said. "We'll tell Zoey tomorrow night when we're both home. Does that work for you?"

It didn't. Not at all. He wasn't ready for Zoey to move, and he had no idea how they were going to explain that he was her biological father. But he found himself nodding anyway. What else was there to do?

She patted his hand, grabbed her beer, and disappeared into the room she shared with Zoey.

He grabbed his own beer and headed for the shower, praying either the hot water or the beer would wash away the tightness in his chest.

CHAPTER 19

*F*aith hadn't slept more than an hour the night before. Between worrying about her dad and fuming about Hunter and her mother, she'd tossed and turned until she'd finally rolled out of bed at a quarter to five.

With nothing else to occupy her mind, she showered and headed to the spa to catch up on admin work. The first thing she noticed when she fired up the computer was the appointment calendar, and her eyes nearly bugged out. Her personal schedule had been cleared for the day, but the rest of the week was booked solid with massages, facials, and mani-pedis. More than half were highlighted in blue, indicating that Vivian had secured the appointments. She wanted to call Vivian to express her appreciation, but it was still way too early. Instead, she made a note to do that later and tackled the unpaid invoices.

She was knee deep in the financials when her cell phone rang. The number indicated it was coming from Eureka, and she answered it immediately. It was the doctor at the hospital. Her father was awake.

Faith quickly stopped at Incantation Café for sugar and caffeine and then got on the road immediately. But the traffic was so bad that it still took her over an hour to get there. By the time she arrived, Clair, her father's girlfriend, was in the waiting room pacing. She'd come to the hospital late the previous evening and had still been there when Faith had left. Faith imagined that she hadn't gotten much sleep either.

Faith gave her a quick hug and asked, "What's going on?"

Anger flashed in Clair's eyes, something Faith rarely saw, and she spat out, "Gabrielle is here again. After twenty years, what makes her think she can just stroll right back into his life? I can't believe she convinced the nurses to let her in. I'm just so mad I could spit. Here I am waiting, while she's in there doing… I have no idea, but he doesn't need this stress. She needs to leave."

Faith couldn't agree more. "I'll take care of it." She hugged Clair one more time and took off down the hall to her father's room. She stood in the doorway and glared at her mother, who was sitting beside Lin's bed, holding his hand. "I thought we told you your presence wasn't welcome," Faith said. "You should leave."

"Faith, it's okay," Lin said, his voice raspy.

Gabrielle Townsend rose from her chair but didn't release Lin's hand.

Faith's eyes narrowed as she stared at their connection. *How dare she?* She strode over to her father's side. "What are you doing here, Gabrielle?" she asked, deliberately not calling her Mom. "What do you and Hunter want from us?"

"Hunter?" she asked, confusion swimming in her blue eyes. "He doesn't know I'm here." She let out a humorless laugh. "If he did, he'd likely be here tossing me out."

"Maybe I should give him a call then," Faith said coldly.

"Faith," her father said again.

She turned her attention to him and felt the anxiety she'd been carrying around since the day before start to drain away. His eyes were bright, and his cheeks were rosy. But more importantly, he no longer looked frail, as if he'd break at any moment. "You scared us, Dad."

"I don't mind telling you I scared myself, baby girl." He reached for her hand. The moment his skin touched hers, she felt the difference. The dread, anxiety, and unease had vanished, and all she felt was extreme fatigue. He wasn't completely out of the woods, but the meds had worked, and her dad was in the process of getting better.

"Don't do that again," she ordered and pressed a kiss to his cheek. When she straightened, she looked at her mother and again asked, "What do you want?"

"Nothing... I just wanted to explain, to make amends, I guess." She turned her head, averting her gaze.

"Faith," her father said gently. "Can you give me and your mother a few minutes? There are a couple things we need to discuss."

"But..." Faith shook her head. Her mother had broken his heart. Broken her four girls' hearts.

"Please," he said. "It will only be a few minutes."

She wanted to scream, but she wasn't going to argue with him. For today, it was enough that he was awake and beating the infection. "All right. But *Clair* and I will be waiting."

"I know Clair's out there. At least I hoped she was." He gave Faith a chagrined smile. "Tell her not to be too angry with me. She's still the only one I'll let steal my morning coffee."

Faith chuckled. "I'll tell her, but I'm not sure your charm is going to work. She's pretty annoyed."

"Don't worry. Clair will forgive me." He kissed the back of her hand and let go. "Five more minutes."

Gabrielle just stood there, staring at her feet.

Faith was disgusted, and the primal anger that had overtaken her earlier in the week came roaring back. She wanted to scream, cry, break things. But she didn't. She kept her head held high and walked back out to the waiting room, where she relayed her dad's message to Clair.

Clair, to her surprise, threw her head back and laughed. "Oh, he knows he's in deep. Share his coffee indeed."

"Inside joke?" Faith asked.

"Something like that."

"So, you're not mad at him?"

Clair frowned. "I was never mad at him, but I'm furious with her. This was not the time for her to just show up out of nowhere. It was already stressful enough for you girls. You don't need her drama, too."

The anger that Faith had been holding down started to fade. Clair was right. They didn't need Gabrielle's drama right then, and Faith had no obligation to spend any energy worrying about it. She leaned back and closed her eyes. In seconds, she was asleep.

"Faith, wake up."

A sharp pain seized Faith's neck as she jerked awake. "Oh, ouch," she said, pressing her hand to her neck as she stretched from side to side. "That was a bad idea."

Clair nudged her and pointed to Gabrielle, who was standing at the nurse's station. She was wearing a long, flowery, faded blue and white skirt and a white fleece jacket with a pair of very worn leather boots. She was neat and clean, but it was clear her clothes were several years old with many miles of wear. And for the first time, Faith could really see how rough her mother's life had been. Hunter had told her, but she hadn't fully understood what that life must've meant for her as well as Hunter.

"Looks like run-away-mommy is done," Faith said, getting to her feet. She glanced at Clair, "Are you coming?"

Clair stared at Gabrielle and shook her head. "You go along. I have something to take care of first."

Faith watched as Clair rose and walked across the room to Gabrielle. After a few words, the pair walked down the hall toward the exit. "Well, that's interesting," she said to no one as she headed back to her dad's room.

He was sitting up, carefully sipping from a paper cup when she returned.

"Hey, baby girl. Come sit with me," he said, patting the edge of the bed.

She did as she was told, and as he draped an arm around her shoulders, she snuggled into him. "Feeling better?"

"Better is an understatement," he said. "The energy potions in this place make me feel eighteen again."

"Is that why you let Mom stay? Nostalgia for the good old days?"

He snorted. "Hardly."

Faith dropped the teasing pretense and looked up at her father. "Then why? It's been twenty years. Why should we listen to what she has to say?"

Lin Townsend brushed a lock of hair out of his daughter's eyes and gave her a gentle smile. "Baby girl, I didn't let her stay for her. I let her stay for me. I wanted answers."

"Did you get them?" she asked.

He shrugged. "Some."

"Did it make a difference?" Faith understood wanting answers, but she was dubious that Gabrielle's revelations would heal any of the wounds her mother had inflicted on all of them, especially her dad, who'd loved her and would've done anything for her.

"It's hard to say. Probably." Lin tightened his hold on his

daughter and said, "I was angry for a very long time, Faith. I don't want that for you."

"It's too late, Dad. I didn't know just how much anger I had until she contacted me. It was as if I'd suppressed all of my feelings when it came to her. She was gone, and as far as we all knew, we'd never see her. But then suddenly there she was, wanting... I don't even know what she wants, but I suspect it's our forgiveness or understanding, and I just don't think I have it in me to get there." She used her thumb to twist the silver ring she wore on her right hand. It had waves carved in the silver, representing her ability to manipulate water. "I lost it the other day. I had a full-blown melt down, and ever since then, I've just been empty. I don't have anything to give her."

"Sure you do, honey. We always have compassion."

"I can't forgive her, Dad. How does any decent person do what she did?" The image of her mom driving away for the last time was right there in Faith's memory. She'd dreamed about it as a kid. In every dream, her mother would turn around and come back to them, the dream ending with her mom engulfing all four of them in a hug and promising to never leave them again. During the hour she'd been asleep the night before, she'd dreamed that same dream again. Only instead of waking up missing her mom, she'd woken up with an icy indifference. She no longer wanted her mother to turn that car around. It was better for everyone if she just stayed away.

"No one says you have to forgive her, Faith," her father said gently. "But if you can find your way to forgiveness, it might help you more than it will her."

"Do you forgive her?" Faith asked.

"I'm getting there, I think." He picked his cup up again and took a sip. "Your mother, well, now that I've talked to her, I've come to the conclusion that she didn't want to leave us but felt she had to."

"Had to? Why? Is she some sort of monster who turns into a psycho killer after midnight? Because otherwise, that sounds like a copout." Faith knew she was being unreasonable, that she should listen to what her father had to say before lashing out, but she couldn't help it. She'd spent twenty years pretending her mother's abandonment hadn't affected her, but it clearly had, and now she was having trouble processing.

"Not exactly," he said frowning. "But in her mind, it was close enough."

Faith sat up and looked her father in the eye. "Does Mom have a mental illness or something?"

He shook his head. "No, baby girl. She's an addict. Potions. She used to make energy potions, and at some point she turned to banned substances to make them stronger and became addicted. The day before she disappeared, she left you in Eureka and couldn't remember where. Do you remember that?"

"What?" Faith frowned, searching her memory. Nothing surfaced. "No."

"She took you to the beach while your sisters were at a birthday party for one of the older kids at school. When she got home, you weren't with her."

Faith blinked. "Where was I?"

He chuckled. "You'd hooked up with a little boy at the beach and built a sand castle. It was well over an hour before his family realized your mom was gone. So they took you out for ice cream and called the sheriff's office, who got in touch with me without much trouble. We picked you up a few hours later. You were fine, but I was furious and your mom, well, she was devastated."

She vaguely remembered going for ice cream after a day at the beach, but the memory was blurry and obviously not a traumatic one for her. "Was that the first time she did something like that?"

"You mean losing one of our children?" His brows drew together, and he got a pained expression on his face. "That was a first. But she had been acting strange, sort of manic depressive, and I'd been asking her to go see someone, but she flatly refused. Now I know it was the potions. She left because she was addicted and didn't want to hurt you or your sisters."

Faith let that piece of news sink in. She had no idea how she was supposed to feel knowing her mother left them for her drug addiction. On the one hand, she was grateful her mother cared enough that she didn't want them subjected to her drugged mental state. On the other, she hadn't loved them enough to try to get help. She'd loved the potions more. "I don't know what to do with that, Dad."

"You don't have to do anything with it, Faith. Just know whatever her faults and issues, she did and still does love you. Addiction is a disease. Try to remember that and maybe someday you'll be able to understand what she did, even if you can't forgive."

"Forgiveness is a hard ask."

"That's why it's more for you than her. If you can let go of the pain, you'll be better for it." He kissed her on the top of her head. "By the way, thank you for what you did for me yesterday."

She jerked back a little, startled. "I didn't do anything other than call 911."

"You did a lot more than that. Your magic, whatever you did... the healer said you helped speed up my healing process. They weren't expecting me to bounce back quite so fast."

"I did?" she asked, still not quite believing it.

"You did. Now go tell Clair I'd like to see her. I think I might have some groveling to do."

Faith laughed. "Yeah, you definitely do. But don't worry, she loves you. She'll get over it soon enough. Just tell her you like her shoes. Girls like that."

He grinned. "Always."

But before Faith could even get to her feet, the door cracked open, and Clair walked in with a smirk on her face.

Faith raised a curious eyebrow. "Did you get that *thing* taken care of?"

Clair gave her a decisive nod and then turned her attention to Lin. "Your ex-wife won't be barging in here again. Not unless she calls first and you decide you want to see her, anyway."

"You saw to that?" Lin asked, sounding surprised.

"Absolutely. Is that a problem?"

"No." He chuckled. "I've said everything I needed to say to her." He held his hand out to her. When she took it, he asked, "Am I forgiven?"

"Yes, but only because you're in the hospital. Do that again and..." She glanced at Faith then leaned down and whispered something in his ear.

Lin winced.

Faith laughed and slipped out, giving them their privacy.

CHAPTER 20

*T*he cold air stung Hunter's skin, but he barely felt it as he hammered nails into the fence he was repairing at the Townsend orchard. The physical labor was welcome after the emotionally draining past few days. It had only taken Vivian half a day to find a house to rent in Eureka. She was already packing her and Zoey's things. Watching his daughter's books go into a box had nearly broken him.

It amazed him how fast he'd gotten attached to her. He'd wanted to grab hold of her and never let go. Instead, he and Vivian had set their daughter down and told her that Hunter was her biological father. She'd taken it in stride, claiming she'd already adopted him, so this just made it official.

He knew she'd have questions later that they'd have to deal with, but for now it had gone far easier than he'd ever expected. But they still needed to work out custody. He'd brought it up again, but Vivian had brushed him off, saying they'd work it out later. The lack of a concrete plan unsettled him, but it had only been a few days. He was trying to be patient.

Unfortunately, patience was something he was running short on. There were two people who were important to him: his daughter and Faith. His daughter was moving forty miles away, and he hadn't seen Faith since the day at the hospital when Gia had shown up uninvited. He'd called her, but she hadn't called back. He'd stopped by her office the night before after finishing her outdoor space, but Lena told him she'd been out all day.

Hunter positioned another nail and swung hard. It went all the way in with the one powerful stroke. He repeated the movement three more times, with each swing growing progressively harder until he misjudged the last one and ended up bending the nail in half. He cursed and started to pull the nail out.

"That's a shame. You were on such a roll," a familiar feminine voice said from behind him.

He lowered the hammer and turned, squinting in the afternoon light. "Faith?"

She slid out of the golf cart and walked over to him, looking so lovely it was all he could do to not reach out and pull her into him. But even though she'd sounded friendly enough in her greeting, her brows were pinched, and her expression had an air of determination. She was there on a mission, and he was certain it had nothing to do with getting closer to him. She stopped a few feet from him and said, "We need to talk."

Hunter placed the hammer in his toolbox and grabbed the jacket he'd draped over the fence railing. "Sure. Want to take a walk?"

She glanced at the golf cart and then back at him. The air was so cold he could see his own breath, but moving would certainly keep them warmer than just sitting in the cart. "Okay."

They started out following the fence line. Faith was bundled in a scarf and a thick jacket, her hands stuffed in her pockets. Her cheeks were pink, and so were the tips of her ears. He had a vision of the two of them sitting by a fire, sipping coffee, and laughing with ease. It was already clear they wouldn't be doing that anytime soon.

"What is it, Faith? There's something wrong. There's been something wrong between us ever since Gia—I mean... Gabrielle showed up." His voice trailed off as he realized his blunder.

She stopped suddenly and stared up at him with accusing eyes.

"You already know, don't you?" he asked.

"What's that? The fact that my mother happens to be your uncle's girlfriend? The one who raised you after your parents' accident? The one you call Gia?"

"So, she finally told you," he said.

"No." She let out a bark of laughter that held no humor. "Funny thing, no one told me. I had to overhear it. Imagine my surprise to find out the guy I'd just started dating, the one I'd spilled my heart to, hid that he not only knew my mother, but knew exactly where she'd been all those years. So while he was drying my tears, he was holding back some pretty pertinent information. I'm here to find out why. So, tell me, Hunter, why did you target me? What was it you and Gabrielle hoped to gain by you coming to work for me? Huh? Why the lies?"

"Whoa." Hunter held his hands up and took a step back, completely taken off guard. "I didn't lie to you, Faith."

"Right." Her eyes were a little wild, and she was so keyed up she was practically shaking. "It just happens to be a coincidence that your guardian was my mother? I don't buy it. What do you want from me?"

He wanted to wrap her in his arms, hold her tightly, and

whisper reassurances, but he was afraid that if he tried to touch her, she'd haul off and deck him. And maybe he'd deserve it. She needed answers, not someone to protect her. "You want to know what I want, Faith? Are you sure you really want to know?"

"Yes." Her answer was defiant and had the air of a challenge.

"Fine. I want you. I want your heart, your friendship, your body, and your soul. I want it all. I want you so bad I ache for you, and I have since the first moment we met."

She opened her mouth, closed it, and then shook her head. She was speechless, exactly the effect he was going for.

"But I already know I can't have any of that because you don't trust me. Under the circumstances, I guess I can understand that. But if you'll give me a chance, I think I can change your mind."

"You can't…" She shook her head again. "You knew Gia was my mother and didn't tell me."

"I didn't know, Faith. I really didn't. Not until late last week when I saw a picture on your desk. That was when I found out. I've only ever known her as Gia, my uncle's girlfriend. I didn't know her real last name was Townsend."

"So you knew when we were on our date?" Her tone was accusatory, and he bit back a wince.

"Yes. I knew then."

"And still, you didn't say anything." She placed her hands on her hips and glared at him. "You let me be blindsided."

He frowned. "That wasn't my intention. I wanted Gia—Gabrielle—to have a chance to tell you herself. That's the only reason I didn't say anything. I knew she was coming on Sunday, but then Lin got sick and she showed up at the hospital like that." Hunter paused, trying to collect his thoughts. "I was angry that she'd do something so inappropriate, so I confronted her about telling you the truth. Obviously she still hasn't, otherwise I doubt you'd be so angry with me right now."

"I overheard the two of you arguing at the hospital," Faith said quietly.

"When we were outside?" That's when it hit him. Her entire demeanor had changed when he'd gone back inside. She'd sent him away and hadn't answered any of his calls. Hunter moved closer and reached for her hand, taking it in his. "I'm sorry, Faith. I can see how you'd think I'd been lying to you. But I swear I wasn't."

She stared at their joined hands. "I guess I could've understood that argument if she wasn't an addict, Hunter. You should've told me before we made plans to meet her."

In that moment, he saw his fatal mistake. He was used to dealing with addicts. His life with Mason and Gia had been one of survival, one Faith and her sisters hadn't needed to learn to navigate. In his desire for her to get her answers, he'd inadvertently let her walk into a dangerous situation or at least a potential one. If Gia had shown up hopped up on her potions, anything could've happened. "I'm sorry, Faith. I went up and saw her on Friday night. She was sober then, doing better than I'd seen in years. If I'd thought she'd be dangerous, I'd have said something."

"My sisters all have little girls to think of," she said.

"I know. You're right, I should've said something. I was just... I saw how much pain you were in. I wanted you to make peace with your mother if for no other reason than for yourself."

She stared at her feet. "My dad said something similar about making peace and figuring out how to forgive. He said it would be better for me, not her. But you know what, Hunter?"

"What's that?"

"I don't have a mother. Not really. She lost herself to the potions years ago. And to make matters worse, she told my dad she left because she was afraid she'd hurt us. I could accept that if she hadn't gone on to raise you. She didn't love us enough to stay, but she was there for you. I don't know what that means. Did she love you more than us? Was she too weak to leave a second time? Or maybe she was so far into her addiction that she couldn't make any decisions. All I know is that my mother left us and raised someone else. And that hurts."

Her words sucker-punched him in the gut. He'd hadn't thought about what it would mean to her that he knew her mother and she didn't.

"I can't be with you, Hunter. Not right now. It's too much for me to process." She reached up and pressed her hand to his cheek. "I know you to be a good man. And I'll probably regret this for a very long time. But we have too many factors working against us. And one you should be giving your full attention to."

"Faith, I—" he started, wanting desperately to change her mind, but she cut him off.

"You need to focus your attention on your daughter, Zoey."

The words hung in the air as they stared at one another. Finally, Hunter said, "You heard that part, too, then?"

She nodded.

"I didn't know. No one did." He explained Craig's blood transfusion and how they finally realized the truth. "We never intended to keep it a secret. We just wanted to tell Zoey first so she wouldn't hear it from someone else."

"I understand," Faith said. "I really do. But I think you need to give Vivian a chance. Not me. See if you can put your family back together, Hunter. Don't you all deserve that?"

Had she really just implied that he should be with Vivian? Were the two of them in cahoots or something? "Vivian and I are never going to be together," he said flatly, tired of having the same argument with all the women in his life. "We aren't a good match."

"What about Zoey? Doesn't she deserve to have both of her parents full-time?" Faith asked earnestly. "Isn't that what we both wanted as kids?"

He ground his teeth together. "I will always be present for my daughter, Faith. That doesn't mean I have to pretend to love someone when I'm in love with someone else."

"Don't... don't do that, Hunter. Don't say things you can't take back."

"Who said I wanted to take it back? It's the truth. You already know how I feel about you."

"And I've already made it clear I can't be with you. Thank you for the work you've done at the spa. It's incredible as always. Since the work is complete, I'll mail you the recommendation you asked for within the week."

"I don't care about the recommendation," he said.

"I'll send it anyway." She turned around and started to head back toward the golf cart. After a few steps, she paused and glanced back. "I really am sorry. I hope you find what you're looking for with someone else."

He didn't respond. He just stood there, his heart turning to stone as he watched the only woman he'd ever wanted walk out of his life.

CHAPTER 21

$\mathcal{L}$incoln Townsend was discharged from the hospital just two days after he'd been admitted. All four sisters and Clair had been there to accompany him home, but Lin wasn't having any of it. Once they got back to the house, he'd ordered everyone out, saying he wasn't dying anytime soon and he wouldn't have his daughters acting otherwise.

After some mild protests, Clair agreed to stay with him for the next few days to keep an eye on him. But even Faith had to agree it wasn't really necessary. The healers were confident he was out of the woods, and his oncologist had said there were no changes in his condition. It appeared, for the time being at least, that Lincoln Townsend was correct, and he wasn't going anywhere.

When Faith walked out onto the front porch, she hadn't been able to ignore Hunter's truck parked off to the side. He was on the property somewhere, taking care of the orchard while Lin was recuperating. She hadn't been able to resist. She needed answers.

And she'd gotten them. As she drove the cart away

from him, her heart felt as if it had shattered into a million pieces. He'd told her he wanted her, heart, mind, body, and soul. If she hadn't been so jumbled inside, so messed up by her mother's choices, she would've thrown herself into his arms and never let go. But she couldn't. It hurt more to be with him than it did to be away from him. So she did the only thing she could do—she made a clean break.

She couldn't remember parking the cart in her dad's garage or how she got into her car, but the next thing she knew, she was driving down her father's mile-long driveway, the twinkle lights on the trees blinding her. She felt empty inside. The emotional overload had drained her, and when she got home, she headed straight for the shower.

When she emerged, she felt like a new woman. Or at least like one who had control of her life again. She'd decided, just like Noel, that she wasn't ready to visit with her mother, although she knew Abby and Yvette were making an effort. Unlike Noel, she was fine with that. They had a right to ask their questions and decide for themselves if Gabrielle should be in their lives. Faith wanted something simpler, no complications. And that's why she decided to keep her date with Brian.

He was fun and uncomplicated. The two things she desperately needed in her life at that moment. She took care to dress up for the date. She wore a festive red dress, her black boots, and a super-soft, handmade, black and red scarf.

It was five minutes till the hour when her doorbell rang. Faith felt a grin spread over her face as she started to open the door. Brian stood on her front porch, freshly shaven and holding a box from A Spoonful of Magic.

"What's this?" she asked, waving him in and taking the gold-wrapped box.

"Just a little something for dessert," he said, following her inside. "I figure if the date goes well, we can share it later."

She raised both eyebrows. "You're counting on getting invited in after dinner?"

He chuckled. "I wouldn't say counting on it, but I like to be prepared."

"Of course you do." She set the box on the counter and then opened it, finding a gorgeous chocolate tart inside. "Oh my. You're vying for date of the year, aren't you?"

It was his turn to raise his eyebrows. "Is that all it takes? A fancy dessert?"

"Sometimes." She laughed, already feeling better about her decision. Closing the lid on the box, she said, "Let's go find out if you're dessert worthy, shall we?"

"Oh, I am. Trust me on this one." He pressed his hand to the small of her back, and when they got to the coatrack beside her front door, he chose the black wool coat she'd planned to wear and helped her put it on. "You look gorgeous tonight. I think I forgot to tell you that."

"So do you," she said, eyeing his dark blue button-down shirt, wool pants, and matching sports coat. She leaned in slightly and added, "You smell really good too."

"You like that? I call it soap," he said with a wink.

She laughed again. "Good to know you like to stay clean. That will help with the after-dinner dessert decision." Her face heated as soon as the words flew out of her mouth, but there was no taking them back, so she just grinned and said, "I hope you make the cut."

"Why, Faith, I do believe you're flirting with me," he said and guided her out the door toward his sleek, black SUV.

"Good, you noticed," she said almost shyly. The date was off to a great start, and she berated herself for canceling on Friday night. If she'd known she'd have this much fun, she might have saved herself some heartache and not fallen so hard for Hunter.

"Faith, I notice everything about you, gorgeous." He opened the passenger door and helped her in.

They talked, laughed, and flirted all the way to Woodlines, the restaurant he'd picked for the evening. Once seated, they ordered wine and the crab cake appetizers. It turned out they both loved shellfish, but not oysters or squid. They also were big fans of Italian, but not Thai. And both of them loved watching basketball, but not baseball.

"I think we might have one or two things in common," Brian said as he tipped his wine glass to hers.

"I think you might be right." She brought her wine glass to her lips, and that's when she spotted Hunter seated across the room with Zoey. The two of them had their heads bent together, and they were laughing with wild abandon. Just hours ago, she'd been sure she'd broken his heart. And now here he was at a nice restaurant, on a father-daughter date, enjoying the hell out of himself. The sight of them nearly broke her heart all over again. Had she really walked away from him? Away from his gorgeous daughter?

"Faith?" Brian asked. "Everything okay?"

"What?" She jerked her attention back to him and nodded. "Sure. Sorry, I got distracted."

His gaze followed hers as she glanced at them once more. "Oh, Hunter and Zoey. They look like they're having a good time."

"They do, don't they?" she agreed.

"That will be me and Skye one day," he said.

She forced herself to focus on her date. "That's right, you thought she was your child for the first nine months of her life, right?"

He nodded, having no reason to hide anything. "Yes, we thought she was mine, but it turns out Jacob is the lucky bastard who gets to pay for her college education instead. I'll just be the one spoiling her with dinners and fun vacations to Disneyland."

It was funny how history kept repeating itself. Jacob and Brian, who were best friends, had been involved with the same woman a few years back, and for a while, Skye's mother had lied to everyone. She'd known all along who Skye's father was, but she'd been having ongoing mental health issues after the birth of her daughter. Eventually everything had worked out, and Jacob now had custody of his daughter. Not long after everything was settled, Brian had moved to Keating Hollow to be close to both of them.

Their situation wasn't exactly the same as Craig and Hunter's, but it was close. Considering how well things were going for them, even though Skye's mother was barely in the picture, it made Faith wonder if she'd been too hasty rejecting Hunter. Did he really need to be with Zoey's mother to be a great father? Faith's own father had raised his girls as a single dad and had been amazing. Why was she so stuck on the thought he should give Vivian a chance? A little voice in her head said, *You aren't. You're just scared.*

"Faith?" Brian said again. "Where'd you go?"

"Huh?" She turned so fast, she knocked her water over. "Oh, no. I'm so sorry."

The waiter came over and quickly cleaned up the mess, but by the time he was done, she was watching Hunter and Zoey again.

Brian let out an audible sigh. "I should've known better."

"Excuse me?" she asked.

"Just tell me one thing," he said, leaning in closer to her.

"What's that?"

"Why did you go out with me if you have feelings for Hunter?"

She blinked at him. Had he really just said that? He had. She opened her mouth to protest but quickly shut it. How could she deny it? Her feelings were probably written all over her face. Instead, she hung her head and said, "I'm sorry, Brian. You're right. I don't want to have feelings for Hunter, but there they are. It's not fair to you."

He smiled at her. "But you do like me."

"I do," she agreed with a nod. "You're fun and easy to be with."

"That's a great combination, but I guess you were never really considering inviting me in for that dessert, were you?"

"Is that all you were interested in, dessert?" she asked with her eyes narrowed.

He flashed her a sexy little half smile. "No, not at all. But when I'm on a date, I sure would like to know it's at least a possibility. If not, then all we're ever going to be is friends. Which is fine of course, but I might not use the fancy soap."

"You're being too kind," Faith said, feeling bad that she'd used him to make her feel better about Hunter.

"Nah. I'm having a good time. I just need to readjust my expectations." He grabbed a forkful of crab cake and shoved it in his mouth.

"Friends it is then," she said and lifted her glass to his. "Do you want the tart back when you drop me off?"

He laughed. "No, Faith. You keep it. I need to watch my manly figure if I'm going to be on the prowl again."

She eyed him and nodded. "You're right. A few more pounds and you'll be laughed right out of the gym. Better leave the tart-eating to the pros."

They joked their way through the rest of the dinner, all while Faith kept an eye on Hunter and Zoey. By the time they left, Faith was certain Brian was on deck to be her new bestie, right behind Hanna. She couldn't believe how easy he was to talk to and how much they made each other laugh. And when he dropped her off, she once again decided it was a shame that the chemistry needed for a romantic relationship just wasn't there.

"Goodnight, Brian. Thanks for dinner. It was wonderful," she said.

"So were you," he said as he leaned over and kissed her cheek. "Do you mind if I give you a piece of advice?"

She stiffened, not sure she wanted to hear what he had to say, but she nodded anyway.

"If you love him, don't let him get away."

"It's... complicated," she said.

He gave her a knowing smile. "Relationships always are, beautiful."

"Yeah, I guess you're right." She opened the door of the SUV and slid out. "Goodnight, Brian. Drive safely."

"Goodnight, Faith. Think about what I said." Then he backed out of her driveway as she watched him go.

Was he right? Should she run back to Hunter and tell him everything she'd said didn't matter? That she loved him, too? The temptation was strong, but she refrained. She still needed to work some feelings out, and she couldn't do that with Hunter clouding her brain.

She was so busy thinking about the chocolate tart, she didn't even notice the shivering woman standing off to the side of her porch until she heard something that sounded like teeth chattering. She glanced over and nearly jumped out of her skin when she found Gabrielle Townsend shivering in the cold night air.

"Mom?" she asked. "What are you doing here?"

"Faith," her mother slurred and grabbed onto Faith's jacket

to keep from falling over. "I missed you, baby. Why don't you let your mommy in and we can talk?"

Faith glared at her. "You're high."

Gabrielle giggled. "Maybe just a bit. It's been a rough few days. I had to do what I had to do."

Disgust rolled through Faith, making her stomach turn. "You need to go. You can't be here."

"But I need a place to sleep," her mother threw one arm in the air. "And your sister Noel won't rent me a room at her inn."

Of course she wouldn't. Noel wasn't going to put up with anyone who was hopped up on elicit potions. Especially since she had Daisy and a new baby on board. She wasn't exactly sure what she should do. If she didn't let her mother in, there was no telling what kind of trouble she'd get into. Not to mention the temperature was supposed to get below freezing that night. She really had no choice. She'd never be able to live with herself if she shut her out and something happened to her.

Faith let out a frustrated sigh, unlocked her door, and invited her mother in.

Gabrielle grinned and planted a wet kiss right on Faith's mouth. "I always knew you were a good girl, Faithie."

Her mother stumbled through the door and promptly vomited all over the tiled entry.

CHAPTER 22

"*S*it here. Don't move," Faith ordered, while her puppy Xena whined from her crate.

"You have the cutest dog," her mother squealed as she started to sink down onto the wooden kitchen chair, but then she thought better of it and moved toward Xena's crate. "You should let her out. Caging animals is cruel, Faith."

"It's not cruel, Gabrielle," Faith said testily, grabbing her by the shoulders just before she released the dog. "It's her safe space. Leave her alone."

"Her safe space," Gabrielle laughed hysterically and draped her entire upper body across her kitchen table. "Nowhere is safe." Then she lifted her head and said, "Your kitchen is so nicccccce. How about you let me move in? I'll cook every day." She snorted. "Or at least every week."

"Goddess above," Faith muttered as she reached down for Xena, scooped her out of her crate and carried her to the back yard to let her do her business. When they returned, Faith grabbed her cleaning bucket, gloves, and supplies from her pantry. "Don't touch anything. I'm going to clean up your mess and then we're going to pour some coffee down your throat."

Gabrielle reached out and poked Faith in the arm. "Oops. No touching."

Faith glared at her but knew her wrath was lost on the doped-out woman. What had she done to deserve this crazy in her life? *Nothing*, she reminded herself. Her mother's actions had nothing to do with her.

Muttering under her breath, she went to work on the mess in her entry. Twenty minutes later, she discarded the gloves, towels, and the mop head into a trash bag and hauled it out to the garbage bin. When she returned, she found Xena sitting under the table, cowering, and her mother passed out on the living room floor, snoring. Faith couldn't help wondering how the heck she'd stumbled into the other room by herself.

"Come here, baby," she said to the dog, picking her up and carrying her back to her crate. "Why don't you just stay in here for now. Seems safer for both of us."

Xena shot back into her crate, making Faith wonder what her mother had done to her to make her so skittish. If she'd hurt Faith's dog, there was going to be hell to pay. "It's okay, girl." Faith tucked a couple of treats into her bowl and scratched behind her ear. "She'll be gone in the morning, and you won't have to deal with her again."

Once the dog was settled, Faith moved back into the living room and eyed her motionless mother. At least Faith wasn't going to have to deal with any more of her crazy for the evening. Concerned the woman would vomit again, she grabbed her by her shoulders and, with considerable effort, managed to haul her onto the couch. After positioning her on her side, Faith draped a blanket over her mother and retreated to her kitchen to put on a pot of coffee. The idea of going to bed while Gabrielle was in the house was out of the question.

If she woke up, Faith had no idea what kind of trouble she'd get into.

When the coffee was done, Faith poured herself a cup, grabbed a copy of the latest Angie Fox paranormal mystery, and settled in her oversize arm chair, prepared for an all-nighter.

FAITH DREAMED she was sunbathing on a tropical island. A breeze wafted through the air, and she lay there basking in the sun, enjoying the warmth that seemed to seep into her bones. *This is so much nicer than the chilly air of the northern California coast in the middle of December,* she thought to herself. She felt like she could say there forever and be perfectly happy.

But then the heat turned intense and she found herself coated in sweat. Her eyes were watering, and she suddenly couldn't breathe.

"Faith! Wake up now, sweetheart. I need you to wake up." The urgency in Hunter's voice pulled her out of her dream. Her eyes flew open, and her dream turned to horror. Fire surrounded her, climbing the walls and licking at her dining room set. The couch across from her was ablaze, and thick dark smoke obscured the rest of her house.

"There you are," he said, his arms held out as he concentrated on the nearest flames, his magic holding them back. "Come on. I need you to get up and follow me."

She squinted, spotted the couch again, and yelled, "Where's my mom?"

"Mom?" He frowned. "Gia was here?"

"Yes!" She jumped up and started to move closer to the couch, but the heat was too intense, and Hunter jerked her back, saving her from a flying ember.

"Faith, no. She's not there. No one's there. We have to get out of here while I can still—" He coughed, and his eyes were red and watering from the smoke.

"Dammit!" she cried and let him pull her from the burning wreckage. Just as he parted the flames consuming the back door, he executed a series of roundhouse kicks to force the metal door to open. The cool air rushed in, causing the flames to burn hotter.

"Go!" he pushed her out the door, his entire body straining with the effort to stave off the flames.

But before she could move, she heard Xena's pathetic bark, and she turned to Hunter with horror in her eyes. "Xena," she cried. "She's in her crate and can't get out."

"I'll get her!" He shoved her back out the door again, making her fall to her knees on the wet grass. When she glanced back, the opening was once again consumed by the flames.

She scrambled away from the house and ran smack into her sister Yvette.

"Thank the gods," Yvette breathed, clutching her sister with one hand while wielding her magic with the other one to keep the flames from moving from her house to the one on the right. "Where's Hunter?"

"He went after Xena. She's in her crate." she choked out, her eyes watering at the thought of losing her little devil dog. Then her fears shifted to Hunter, and she willed him to burst out of the house.

"Anyone else in the house?" Yvette asked as Drew and Noel ran up to them.

"Mom's in there!" Faith cried, just as Noel crushed her in a hug.

"Mom?" Yvette asked. "No, she isn't. She's the one who called in a panic to say your house was on fire."

"She did?" Faith asked, but she wasn't paying attention as Yvette said something about calling Hunter and Drew. All she could think about was Hunter and Xena in the blazing house. If he didn't get out soon—

The flames claiming the back door finally parted, and Hunter came stumbling out with Xena under one arm twisting frantically to get out of his grip. The moment his feet hit the grass, Xena escaped and ran across the yard, disappearing behind the neighbor's bushes.

"Thank the gods," Faith said and rushed into Hunter's arms. "Thank you," she sobbed into his soot-covered shirt.

He held her tight for just a moment, then kissed her on the head. "You need to let me go, love. There's still work to do."

She immediately jumped back and watched as Yvette and Hunter battled the flames, keeping them contained so that they didn't jump to the nearby houses or the redwoods just beyond the yard.

"What happened?" Noel asked, pulling her further from the fire.

"I don't know." Faith shook her head. "I came home from dinner and found Mom on my front porch, high as a kite. I didn't know what to do, so I let her in."

"You let her in while she was high?" Noel asked, the disapproval in her tone unmistakable.

"What else was I going to do, Noel? Let her freeze?"

"You could've called Drew," she said.

"And then what? He'd put your mom in jail?" Faith asked and then bent over and coughed.

"Better than letting her burn your house down!" Noel stalked off.

Faith sank to the ground and watched her go. Then she turned her attention to her house and barely noticed the tears streaming down her face. It had been her first house. She'd put a ton of sweat equity into fixing the place up, and now... now it was nothing. Just ash and soot.

Had her mother started the fire? She had no idea. Had she left the coffee pot on? It could've been Faith's fault. Or an electrical issue. Or even a lightning strike. Judging by the wet grass, it had rained recently.

"Faith?" Drew said.

She glanced up and spotted her soon-to-be brother-in-law. "Yeah?"

"You should go around to the front of the house and wait for the healer. Gerry Whipple is on her way. She'll check you out and see if you need to go to the hospital."

"Okay." She let him help her up, and he pointed her toward the side of the house that wasn't yet in a full blaze.

"I'm checking the perimeter. I'll meet you over there," he said.

She nodded distractedly and started to make her way toward the narrow pathway between the redwoods and her house. But just as she reached the edge of her yard, an explosion came from the back of the house that sent part of the roof heading straight into the trees.

A loud yelp sounded, followed by Xena shooting out of the trees and straight into the side door that led to the garage.

"Xena! No," Faith started to run after her, but she tripped over one of the pavers she'd put down last year and fell, twisting her ankle. A distinct *snap* filled her ears as she landed, and she knew without a doubt that she'd just broken something. "Xena!" she called again, as she tried to push herself up. But the moment she tried to move, intense, mind-numbing pain shot from her ankle, rendering her helpless.

"Help!" she called, but her cries were drowned out by the fire blazing before her.

Then, as if she were in a horror movie, the worst happened.

A little girl shot out of the trees, her lips forming the word *Xena*, and followed the dog straight into the burning garage.

"Zoey, noooooo!" Faith cried, her head spinning as adrenaline took over. No one was coming. No one could hear her. The fire was raging too loud. It was up to Faith to get Zoey out of the house. By the sheer will of a desperate woman, she managed to get herself up, but the moment she stepped down on her injured foot, she collapsed again, the pain so severe this time that her world turned black.

Faith didn't know how long she'd been out, but she woke disoriented, her entire body shaking with shock.

Zoey. The image of the girl running into the garage came back to her, and this time she started to crawl, inching forward so slowly she thought she'd never get to the side door. Where was everyone? Why had no one come for her? And why was Zoey even there? The questions rattled through her head as she forced herself to move, to get to Hunter's little girl.

Her heart was breaking. Time seemed to stand still even as the fire raged around her. She was hot, knew the fire was close, and hated herself for being so weak. Fifteen more feet to the door. Ten, five, she was almost there.

Kaboom!

Fire rained around her, and she let out a blood curdling scream just as a figure cloaked in a blanket burst from the side door and ran past her toward the backyard. Just before they turned the corner, the singed blanket fell, and Faith let out a gasp.

Gabrielle was carrying a terrified Zoey, who had Xena clutched in her small hands.

CHAPTER 23

Faith sat in the back of Hunter's truck with her foot propped up on his toolbox and Xena on her lap, watching as Drew secured Gabrielle with handcuffs. Abby and Noel stood next to her, both of them silent. Yvette, Wanda, and Hunter were still containing the fire, while Hanna and a few other water witches were doing their best to douse the flames.

"What did she do wrong?" Zoey asked. She was perched on the back of Hunter's truck next to Faith as Gerry Whipple bandaged a minor burn on her arm.

"She made a mistake, sweetie," Faith said. "One that put all of us in danger and caused a lot of damage."

A fat tear rolled down Zoey's face, and her lower lip trembled. "Am I going to be arrested?"

"What?" Faith reached out and took Zoey's uninjured hand in hers. "Why would you think that?"

"I made a mistake, too. I was supposed to stay in the truck. But I saw Xena run out of the woods and went after her. After I got her, I was trying to get back into the truck, but she got away from me and we ended up back in the woods and then the house. She could've been hurt." She stared at the dog, more tears streaming down her face.

"Oh, honey, no. You were a hero. You saved her. It's not your fault she ran into danger," Faith reassured her. Now was not the time to remind her she should not have run into a burning building. That could come later, though who was Faith kidding? She would've done the same thing to save Xena from the fire.

"I don't want to be arrested," Zoey said haltingly as a sob got caught in her throat.

Noel moved to sit next to her and wrapped her arms around the little girl. "No one is going to arrest you, baby. You're safe now. We're all safe now."

Faith gulped, trying to swallow her emotion. She'd learned that when Gabrielle alerted Yvette to the fire, Yvette had called Hunter immediately. He was the fire witch who lived closest to Faith, and he'd been first on the scene. The only problem was he'd had Zoey, and Vivian had already moved to Eureka. There hadn't been time for him to find someone to watch her, so he'd brought her along and had given her strict orders to stay in the truck. She'd only been trying to save Xena.

"Come on, sweetheart," Gerry Whipple said to Zoey. "Let's get you some water. I might even have something sweet for you to suck on." The healer led the little girl over to her car where her supplies were stashed, leaving the sisters alone.

The three of them watched Drew put their mother in the back of his SUV.

"What's going to happen to her?" Abby asked.

Noel shrugged. "Does it matter?"

Both Faith and Abby turned to stare at their sister.

"What? She tried to roast a whole unopened bag of marshmallows on Faith's gas stove and ended up setting her house on fire. The woman almost got our baby sister and her dog killed. Am I really supposed to feel sorry for her because she might go to jail?"

"No," Abby said. "But it sure seems like treatment would be better than confinement."

"She could've gone to treatment at any time in the last twenty years," Noel said. "She chose not to."

"Noel is right," their dad said, walking up to them and sliding an arm around Faith's shoulders. "I would've helped her if she'd just asked."

She glanced up and reached out to hug him, a sob getting caught in her throat. They held on to each other for a long time until they heard the sirens. The firetrucks from Eureka had arrived and took over the firefighting. Drew took off to deliver Gabrielle to the county jail, and after what seemed like forever, Hunter finally strode over, looking for his daughter.

"Zoey? Where is she?" he asked.

"With Gerry Whipple." Faith pointed to the healer's car where the two were waiting for Hunter.

He nodded and strode off.

Faith sighed wistfully as she watched him scoop his daughter up in his arms and hug her as if he wasn't ever going to let go.

"You love him," Abby said quietly.

Faith just nodded. She didn't have the energy to fight it anymore. What was the point? After a night of watching her life go up in flames, everything else just seemed trivial.

"Then do yourself a favor and don't push him away anymore." Abby leaned over and kissed her sister on the head just as Hunter returned with Zoey in his arms. "Ready, Faith?"

"Where are we going?" she asked as she watched her house continue to burn.

"Hospital. We need to get that ankle fixed up."

"But my house..." Gerry had supplied her with a potion

that had numbed the pain, and in her shock, she'd almost forgotten she'd more than likely broken the damn thing.

"It's gone, love," he said gently. "No sense in torturing yourself by watching it turn to rubble. Come on. Let me take you to Eureka."

An ambulance had arrived with the firetrucks, but she was in no hurry to take a ride in one. Better to let them stay and be available for the firefighters if they needed it. "Okay."

"Wait here." He carried Zoey to the cab of the truck, got her settled, and then returned for Faith and Xena. "Ready?"

She nodded.

"Hold on to Xena." Then he reached over and picked her up with ease. A minute later, they were all piled in the truck, headed to the hospital with Faith's foot resting on the dashboard and Zoey clutching the puppy she'd saved.

Exhaustion settled in Hunter's bones as he carried his sleeping daughter into his small cottage. After settling her in the new bed he'd just gotten for her, he made his way back out to the living room where Faith was balancing on crutches, her little dog sitting calmly at her feet.

He gave her a tired smile. "I thought you said your dog was a holy terror."

"She is. I think she's just exhausted like the rest of us."

"She looks more like she's keeping an eye on you," he said as he took the crutches from her.

"Hey! How am I going to get around?" she asked, reaching for them.

"You're not. You're going to bed and elevating that foot like the healer ordered."

"But—"

He once again scooped her up, and even as she protested, he carried her into his bedroom and laid her on the giant king-size bed. Then he reached for Xena, who'd followed them, and placed her on the bed, too. The shih tzu turned around three times and then snuggled up next to Faith, resting her head on her mistress's belly.

If Faith hadn't known his aesthetic due to his help with the spa, she might have guessed he'd hired a decorator. The room was masculine but with just enough soft touches to make it elegant. His bedroom set was painted black, while his bedding was black and gray with plenty of pillows and a turquoise throw blanket folded at the end. There was a black, gray, and turquoise splatter painting on the wall that went perfectly with his turquoise lamps on both nightstands. It was just enough color so that the space didn't feel cold.

Hunter grabbed a couple of the decorative pillows and gently lifted her leg, placing the soft props beneath her foot. "How's this?"

"Fine, but you're not going to make me sleep in my clothes, are you?" Her lips twitched with amusement.

He raised one eyebrow. "Thinking of sleeping in the nude? I wouldn't mind, but—"

"Not tonight." She gestured to her foot. "No strenuous activity for a while, remember?"

"Unfortunately." He grinned at her and then rummaged around in his dresser until he found two sets of sweats and T-shirts. He handed one pair to Faith. "For you to sleep in. Do you need help, or do you think you can manage?"

"I just need help getting into the bathroom." She nodded to her broken foot that was now set in a cast. "Someone took my crutches."

"Not a problem." He carefully carried her into the bathroom and set her on the counter. "I'll be right back with your crutches." A minute later, he handed her the crutches and said, "There's an extra toothbrush in the drawer to the left."

"Thanks," she said.

"No problem at all." He closed the door, grabbed his clothes, and went to get ready for bed in the second bathroom.

When he returned, he found her already under the covers, her casted foot poking out from under the blankets. He helped get her foot repositioned on the pillows and then sat down gingerly and brushed her hair back. "Are you doing okay? Is this comfortable?"

"Yes, but you know I could've just gone to my dad's house. There's plenty of room there."

He sucked in a breath and let it out slowly as he shook his head. "No, Faith, I couldn't have let you go there tonight. Do you know what it did to me when I learned you were in that burning house?" His eyes misted as he added, "When I got the call that your house was on fire and no one was there to help you?"

Her own eyes stung with unshed tears. "I guess I can imagine."

"My heart was in my throat, and I was dying inside, going insane to get to you. And then when I ran inside and found the flames had already trapped you in that living room, I nearly lost my goddamned mind. The idea of being away from you for even a minute is impossible. If I'd taken you to your father's house, he'd have two more extra guests because I wouldn't have been able to bring myself to leave."

She reached up and ran her fingertips over his stubbled jaw. "It would've been fine for you and Zoey to stay there."

"Perhaps. But here I can hold you all night long and not feel guilty about it." He grinned down at her.

"You seem awfully sure of yourself," she said. "Aren't you afraid of taking advantage of a vulnerable woman?" She'd meant the words to be playful, but instead they sounded serious, like she was questioning his motives.

His smile vanished, and suddenly his heart was thundering in his chest. "Faith, I..." He pressed a hand to his forehead and closed his eyes. When he opened them again, he was looking at her as if he was searching her soul. "I know you think I should be trying to have a relationship with Vivian, but—"

"I don't. Not anymore," she said, cutting him off. "That was my stupid insecurity talking. You were right. You can't force something you don't feel, and you shouldn't try."

He blinked, surprised by her one-eighty turnaround. "When did you decide this?"

She let out a short laugh. "Tonight. I had a date with Brian and—"

"You were on a date?" Jealousy snaked through him, and his stomach soured at the thought of her in another man's arms.

"Yes, and we were at Woodlines. I saw you and Zoey having such a good time... and I don't know. I was sad that I wasn't part of it. My date, Brian... he noticed and told me it wasn't fair to lead him on when I was in love with someone else."

Hunter's heart was caught in his throat again. Had he heard her right? "And you said?"

"I told him he was right. It wasn't fair." Her expression softened as she gazed up at him. "I realized then that I was out with the wrong man and that I pushed you away because I was scared. I'm sorry, Hunter. I was angry at my mother and took a lot of it out on you. I shouldn't have done that."

His heart melted when he saw the vulnerability swimming in her gorgeous blue eyes. "It's okay. I have big shoulders, and if you need me to carry your burdens sometimes, I can do that. I'd be happy to in fact."

"It's not your job to do that," she said, shaking her head.

"What if I want it to be?" He bent his head and kissed her

softly on the lips. "What if I want to help carry your load for the rest of our lives?"

Her breath hitched as tears rolled down her temples. "Why would you want to do that? You have your own demons to wrestle with."

"Our demons are the same, sweetheart. Don't you see that? Both of us lost a lot when we were just kids. I've mostly come to terms with my situation. But you... you're still working through it. Working through how you're going to handle Gia—Gabrielle. I'd like to be here for you to lean on if you'll have me."

"I'll definitely have you. But I have to warn you, I think I'm going to be a mess for a while when it comes to my mother. She..." Faith squeezed her eyes shut for a moment. When she opened them, there was raw pain radiating back at him. "She came back, acting as if she was trying to put her life right. But the first thing she did was get high and burn my house down. How do I deal with that? I have no idea."

He ached for her and knew it would be a long time before she came to terms with who her mother had turned into. He knew Gia as a tender-hearted woman who was also selfish. She didn't love herself enough to seek treatment. And no matter how much someone wanted to help an addict, if they didn't want the help, there was nothing anyone could do. "Well, for starters, you and Xena can stay here while I rebuild your house. Your insurance money should be enough to cover the materials, and the advantage of being my girl is that it means I'm free labor. Or we can build a bigger one with more bedrooms."

"More bedrooms?" she asked, blinking at him.

He chuckled. "You know, just in case somewhere down the road we want to fill them with more kids."

She laughed. "You're getting way ahead of yourself, buddy."

"Perhaps, but I like to be prepared." He was certain he was saying way too much way too soon, but after the night's events, he just couldn't manage to hold back. And he didn't want to. "Faith, I think you must know by now, but in case you don't... I love you. I've never told a woman that before, but I'm saying it to you. And I'll love you for the rest of your life if you'll let me."

"Woah," she said softly.

Fear started to creep into his gut as he waited for her to say something else. But he didn't regret laying it all out there. Not after the night they'd had. After his parents died, he'd spent way too many years guarding his heart. He was done with that now.

"You know what?" Faith asked, a slow smile claiming her lips.

"No, what?"

"You're a little crazy." Her eyes glittered with amusement.

"Maybe, but I'm guessing anyone who has three older sisters and a devil dog might be a little crazy, too."

Faith glanced down at Xena, who was snoring lightly. "She looks pretty tame to me."

"So do you on most days," he teased.

Still smiling, she reached up and placed her hand on the back of his neck, pulling him down so that his lips were so close he could feel her breath on them. "I love you, too, Hunter McCormick. Now kiss me."

He didn't hesitate. He closed the distance and kissed her tenderly, all of his love pouring out of him. She was everything he'd ever wanted and everything he'd never known he needed. And in that moment, he knew that whatever came their way, he'd be right by her side until the very end. When he pulled away, silent tears were rolling down her temples again. "Hey," he said softly. "What's wrong, love?"

"Nothing. Nothing at all," she said, shaking her head. "I'm just overwhelmed. Happy and overwhelmed."

"Aww, Faith." He crawled onto the bed, stretched out next to her, and gathered her in his arms, spooning her with her back pressed to his chest. They lay together like that, with Hunter soothingly running his fingers over her arm, until they heard the pitter pat of feet on his wood floors.

"Daddy?" Zoey said, her voice cracking.

He sat straight up. "What is it, Zoey? Are you okay, baby?"

"Can I sleep in here?"

"Of course." He scooted away from Faith, leaving enough room for Zoey to crawl between them. She settled in right next to Faith, sharing her pillow. Faith didn't hesitate to wrap an arm around her and cuddle Zoey to her.

Hunter felt like his heart was going to explode with all the love pouring from him.

Faith glanced up at him. "Ready to turn out the light?"

"Definitely." He reached over, flipped the switch, and then cuddled his two best girls until the sun came up.

CHAPTER 24

"So," Yvette said as she sat down next to Faith. "You and Hunter are just living together now?"

Faith shoved a piece of Noel's bridal shower cake into her mouth and nodded.

Yvette tossed her dark hair over her shoulder and laughed. "Just like that? Your house burns down, so you shack up with the first eligible bachelor you find?"

"Not the first one," Faith said, taking her sister's needling in stride. "I could've imposed on Brian, I guess."

"So many men, so little time," Yvette said with a fake sigh.

They both cracked up.

"Hey, hey, no having fun without me," Abby said, joining them. She was holding a wine bottle that had an actual wine glass attached at the top. "Did you see these?" She held the contraption up. "Saves time. No need for refills."

Yvette grabbed it out of her hand and took a long drink.

"Hey! That's my bottle." Abby snatched it back and held it with both hands, snarling at Yvette like a dog guards his food bowl. "I won that playing the romantic movie quote game."

"Nice, Abs. Good thing Clay can't see how *unsexy* you are right now."

"Clay always thinks I'm sexy." She shimmied her shoulders, making her boobs jiggle.

Everyone laughed. Faith's heart was full of love for her sisters. They were at Noel's wedding shower and the day had been full of pure joy. Yvette had done a fabulous job with the store, making it elegant with a silver and blue winter theme. Hundreds of candles had been enchanted to float in the store, each of them flickering with soft flames, while snow fell from the ceiling then disappeared into thin air before it settled on anyone. It was gorgeous and magical and perfect.

Abby held the wine bottle up. "Cheers!"

Yvette and Faith picked up their regular wine glasses and toasted her. "Cheers!" they said in unison.

"Time for gifts!" Hanna called from across the room.

They watched as Noel opened everything from a fancy can opener to slutty crotchless panties. When she held up the underwear, Faith called out, "She clearly doesn't need those. Drew's already figured out how to get past the modest ones."

Noel smirked at her sister and pressed a hand to her abdomen while everyone laughed and toasted to her pregnancy.

"I think we'll probably still figure out a use for these," Noel said, folding the naughty underwear and putting them with the rest of her haul.

Two pieces of cake later, Faith found herself sitting alone in one of the overstuffed chairs while Abby and Yvette helped Noel load her shower presents into her SUV. She reached down and started to massage her aching calf just above her cast.

"Hey, gorgeous," Hunter said as he sat down next to her. "You doing okay?"

Faith yawned. "Just a little tired."

"That's to be expected while the bone heals," he said, taking her hand.

"That's what they tell me." She smiled at him but then frowned when she saw the tension in his jaw. "What's wrong?"

"I heard from Mason. Gia contacted him. It sounds like she's trying to get a plea deal that will sentence her to treatment and probation instead of jail time."

"No jail time?" Noel asked incredulously. She'd just walked back into the store with Abby and Yvette. "Are you talking about our mother?"

Hunter nodded.

"She has to serve time," Noel insisted. "She almost got people killed."

"Noel," Abby cut in. "Do you really think sending her to prison is going to change anything?"

"It'll keep her off the streets." Noel's expression was set into a hard line as she added, "What if she knocks on Faith's door and prays on her sympathies again? Or if she hurts someone else? No. Treatment isn't enough."

"Noel," Yvette said. "Maybe we should get Faith's opinion since she's the one who lost her house."

They all turned and stared at Faith.

She blinked and shook her head, trying to clear her thoughts. Then she turned her attention to Hunter. "Is treatment instead of jail time even a possibility?"

"It is if you give a sworn statement that you believe the fire was an accident."

"It was reckless, and she was high!" Noel said.

"It was," Faith agreed, nodding at Noel. "No doubt about it. But you don't really think she meant to burn down my house, do you?"

"Of course not," Noel said. "No one tries to burn a house down with marshmallows."

"No one competent anyway," Yvette said under her breath.

Despite the serious nature of the conversation, Faith chuckled. "I wouldn't think so."

"This isn't funny." Noel crossed her arms over her chest and sank into a nearby chair.

"It's not," Hunter said, taking Faith's hand and crouching down beside her. "What do you think, Faith? Whatever you decide, I'm behind you."

She squeezed his hand, wondering what she'd done to deserve a man so devoted to her. "You have a say in this too. Zoey was…" She frowned, unable to even say the words. "I wasn't the only one in danger."

"No, you weren't. But she did run into that burning building to save Zoey when she saw her dart in there. That counts for something," Hunter said.

"Take Zoey out of the equation for a moment," Faith said to Hunter. "If she'd just burned my house down and nothing else happened, what would you say then? You actually know her better than any of us."

Hunter glanced around at the four Townsend sisters, and Faith could tell that he was uncomfortable with the question, but she really wanted to know what he had to say.

She squeezed his hand. "Please, Hunter?"

"Yeah," Abby chimed in. "I want to know, too."

"Same," Yvette said.

He glanced at Noel.

She reluctantly nodded. "Yeah, I guess."

Hunter ran a hand through his hair and then let out a deep sigh. "I know Gia to be loving when she isn't high, and extremely selfish when she is. I don't know how to judge if she deserves to do time. She's two different people. If she had the ability to stay clean, then no. If she doesn't..." He shrugged. "That's up to law enforcement."

"Could you forgive her?" Faith asked.

He stared at her with hardened eyes. "Honestly? No. She put the two people I love most in mortal danger. Addiction or not, actions have consequences. And while I hope she gets better, for her sake and everyone's around her, forgiveness isn't something she deserves from me. It's something she'll need to earn, and from where I'm sitting, I'm not sure she can."

"Dammit," Noel said and turned to Faith. "Why did you have to pick someone so mature? Here I was harboring the biggest freaking grudge on the west coast, and he just put a pin in it. Do what you feel is right. I'll stay out of it."

"Wow. We're never going to hear that again," Abby said. "Can we write that down?"

"Shut it, Abs," Noel said. "I'm not in the mood."

"This will help." Abby handed her another piece of cake.

Noel gave her the tiniest of smiles and shoved a forkful of cake into her mouth.

"I'm for whatever you think is right, too," Abby said, and Yvette nodded her agreement.

"Great. Thanks guys," Faith said sarcastically. "Just leave it all up to me."

They all chuckled while she buried her head in her hands. When she finally came up for air, she said, "I want to see her first."

FAITH AND HUNTER sat across from Gabrielle in the visiting room of the county jail. She was dressed in a blue uniform that resembled scrubs, and she had bags under her eyes.

"Suffering withdrawals?" Hunter asked without an ounce of sympathy.

"I'm so sorry, Hunter," she said, trying to reach for his hand.

He pulled away and gave her a blank stare as he said, "I've heard that before."

"I know. You have no reason to forgive me," she said, sounding so pathetic that Faith wanted to cry. Not for her, but for the loss of the mother she'd known and loved all those years ago.

"You're right. I don't," he said. "But you probably need to learn to forgive yourself before you ask that of anyone else. We're not here to absolve you of your sins."

She tilted her head and gave him a curious look. "Why are you here?"

He jerked his head toward Faith. "She wanted to see you."

Gabrielle turned her attention to Faith, and tears instantly filled her eyes. "I'm so, so sorry, Faith. Your house—" A sob got caught in her throat, and Faith didn't really feel anything. Just pity.

"It can be rebuilt," she said.

"But you could've been hurt, and Zoey..." She glanced at Hunter again. "I'd die if anything ever happened to your little girl."

"So would I," Hunter said.

"Gabrielle," Faith said, "I really only have one question for you."

A pained expression crossed her features as she said, "You can call me mom if you want."

Faith frowned and shook her head. "You haven't been a mother to me for a very long time. I don't think that's appropriate."

"Right. Of course. Gabby is fine. Or Gia," she said, glancing at Hunter again. But he was staring over her shoulder, not making eye contact. Faith couldn't blame him. 'Gia' actually had been a mother figure to him, but she had still failed miserably. It was amazing he had it in him to even make the trip to visit her.

"Okay, Gia, I want to know why you want to go to treatment now when you've refused for the past twenty plus years. Is it only because you're facing jail time, or do you actually want to get clean?"

She sucked in a sharp breath and then blinked rapidly as tears fell silently down her gaunt cheeks.

Faith was unmoved. "Please answer the question honestly. I doubt it's going to change my decision about my statement to the police, but I really want to know."

She wiped away her tears and sniffed. Staring down at her hands, she said, "I won't lie. I'm terrified of going to prison."

"That's understandable," Faith said.

Her mother nodded. "It's also true that I never sought treatment. I wanted to sometimes. I tried to quit on my own sometimes, too. Hunter knows. He's seen the cycle. This last time, I really thought I might make it. I'd been clean for months. But then I saw you girls and... things got really hard."

Hunter looked at Faith and nodded. "That's true. She did try several times."

"We didn't have the money for a fancy rehab center, and to be totally honest, I didn't really want to quit then. Not forever anyway. Not enough to swallow my pride and ask for help. But when I saw that baby run into your burning house, something broke in me. I was still half out of my mind on the potion, but I saw her and knew if I didn't do something..." She paused and swallowed hard, seemingly unable to finish her sentence.

Straightening her shoulders and staring Faith in the eye, she continued, "By the grace of the gods, I managed to get her out, and in that moment when I knew she was safe, I promised myself I'd find help this time. One way or another, I want and need help to get clean. The thought of Zoey... it's unthinkable."

Faith held her gaze, wondering why the woman hadn't felt the same way when Faith had been asleep in the chair. She wasn't really all that hurt by her mother's lack of concern for her. It was obvious her mother was broken in ways Faith couldn't understand. She was just sad. "Is that all?"

She shook her head, the tears coming faster. "I hate myself for what I did to you, Faith. You were my baby, the one I always thought I might be able to come back to. You were so little, so sweet, so pure. I just..." She covered her eyes with her hand. "I ruined everything and destroyed everything you own. Almost destroyed you," she forced out, her voice barely audible. "I don't know how I'll ever forgive myself."

Faith stared at her for a long moment. Then she stood and said, "You'll work on it in treatment." Holding her hand out to Hunter, she added, "Good luck, Gia. I hope you find the strength to get well."

Hunter took her hand, and the two of them walked out of the visiting room. Faith stopped to sign her statement, and then they were back on the road. She turned to Hunter. "Do you think she'll be able to stick with it?"

He shrugged. "I hope so, for her sake."

"Me too." Faith held his hand, and deep down she prayed her mother would get well. No matter what had happened in the past, she hoped someday to know the person her father had fallen in love with all those years ago. Until then, she had plans of her own.

When they entered the town limits of Keating Hollow, Faith said, "Can we go by my house?"

Hunter glanced over at her. "Why? It's all gone, Faith. We already searched for anything salvageable. All that is left is destruction."

"I know. I want to see it anyway."

He gave her a skeptical look but turned the truck in the direction of her former home.

She reached over, grabbed his hand, and squeezed. "Thanks."

The closer they got to her house, the calmer she felt. She'd already had her dad drive her by the remnants of her cottage earlier in the week. Even though she'd known what to expect, it had been a shock to her system, and she'd given herself the afternoon to cry, to let it all out. Then she'd cleaned herself up and let it go. It was just a structure. It could be rebuilt. Her pictures and mementos, those were another thing entirely. She knew it would take time to get over the loss, but she'd already settled on a way forward.

Hunter pulled his truck to a stop in the driveway and killed the engine. Turning to her, he asked, "How did it get cleared so soon?"

The lot was empty, and the only evidence of the burned structure was the scorched earth. "Jacob called in a favor with the contractor who built his house. They came out yesterday and razed it."

"Okay, but why the rush? I was going to line someone up after the new year."

"Let me show you." She pushed her door open and hopped down onto her good foot.

Hunter was out of the truck and around to the passenger side handing her crutches to her before she could even reach into the bed for them.

"Thanks." She made her way over to where her house had once stood and stopped roughly where her bedroom used to be. Pointing one of her crutches toward the back, she said, "I was thinking a nice big en suite bathroom should go here, complete with a walk-in shower and a spa tub for two."

He grinned down at her. "I like the sound of that."

She moved a few paces. "This is the walk-in closet."

"Naturally," he agreed.

She led him around the area, describing what she wanted the kitchen to look like, where the gas fireplace would be in the living room, the large laundry room, and a separate family room. Then she made her way down the area where the hallway would be. "And here, Hunter, I think we'll add three extra bedrooms and an office."

"Three extra bedrooms?" he asked, stunned. "And an office? For me or you?"

"The office is for both of us if you think you can share."

He wrapped his arms around her and stared down into her sparkling eyes. "I can share. Hell, I'm happy to share. Any extra hours of the day with you are more than welcome."

She smiled up at him. "I feel the same way."

"But three extra bedrooms? What are you going to do with those? Open a bed and breakfast?"

She laughed. "I don't think Noel would appreciate the competition." She tightened her hold on him. "No. One is for Zoey, and I think we'll fill the other two with a brother and a sister. Or two brothers or two sisters. Whichever way works out."

"Brother and sister?" he repeated.

"I'm not picky. Girls, boys, one of each." She shrugged, enjoying the look of wonder lighting up his face. "Just as long as they're ours. What do you think?"

He bent his head and claimed her lips in a searing kiss, holding her tight as if he'd never let go. And when he finally came up for air, he said, "I think maybe it's time to get started on filling those bedrooms."

She laughed. "I'm game. Can we wait until we get back to your house, though?"

"Hmm. That's a lot to ask, gorgeous."

"It just gives you something to look forward to," she said and started to hobble back to the truck. But before she could take two steps, he came up from behind and said, "Hold on to those crutches."

"Why?"

"You're taking way too long." Then he hauled her into his arms and carried her to the truck. Once they were inside, he said, "I love the hell out of you, Faith Townsend."

"That's a good thing, because I'm planning on marrying you next summer out on that gorgeous patio you built at the spa. Are you game?"

"You bet your ass. Now tell me you love me."

She slid over the seat until she was right next to him and then whispered, "I love the hell out of you, too, Hunter McCormick. Now hurry up. We have a date in your bedroom."

He gave her a wicked grin and stepped on the gas.

CHAPTER 25

*H*anna Pelsh sat at a table at the reception of Noel and Drew's wedding and watched as Rhys and Lena swayed to the music on the dance floor. Seeing them together reminded her of another wedding almost a year ago at the same Townsend orchard when she'd been the one in his arms. They'd been on three dates and attended Abby and Clay's wedding together, and then he'd given her the talk. The one that started with "We're better as friends" and ended with him brushing her off for the next twelve months.

If she hadn't loved him almost her entire life, she'd have hated him. Now he was dating Faith's receptionist at the spa, and Hanna wondered if seeing them together would actually kill her. Her heart certainly hurt enough.

"Hey!" Faith said as she hobbled over on her crutches and smoothly slid her way into one of the chairs. "What are you doing here all alone, no cake or wine in sight?"

"You're getting really good with those things," Hanna said as she gestured to her empty cake plate. "That was slice number two."

"Damn, I'm falling behind." She waved to Hunter, who was over by the bar, and gestured for two glasses of champagne for her and Hanna and then pointed to the cake table, again holding up two fingers.

Hanna gave her a side-eye glance. "Did you really just order him to get us drinks and more cake?"

"Ordered is a little harsh. More like requested." She grinned, her eyes sparkling with so much happiness it actually helped lift the gloom cloud hovering over Hanna's head. "Can you believe this?" Faith said, waving a hand around at the spectacular decorations. "It's freakin' incredible. Yvette and Abby outdid themselves."

They really had. There were no less than two dozen Christmas trees, each decorated with enchanted white papier-mâché birds, sparkling glass icicles, and twinkling frosted snowflakes. Tinkling wedding bells were perched at the top of each one. There were miniature ice-sculpture snowmen and penguins in the middle of each table, and an enchanted sleigh with reindeer flew overhead, delivering novelty Christmas gifts to all the guests.

Even the champagne seemed extra bubbly. Or maybe Hanna was just extra tipsy. She'd had a few more than usual.

"You're not still pining for Rhys, are you?" Faith asked.

"What?" Hanna jerked her attention to her friend. "I don't pine."

Faith placed a hand over her best friend's and said, "I'm sorry, sweetie, but you do, and you are."

"I hate pining," Hanna said, venom in her tone. "And I hate him for making me feel this way."

"I know. You're very good at hiding it." Faith glanced over at Rhys and Lena. They appeared to be having a disagreement of some sort, but they were keeping their voices down, careful to not make a scene. "Is he still avoiding you?"

"Usually." Hanna shrugged. "The only time he doesn't is when we find ourselves alone. Like if he's the only customer in the café or I'm the only customer in the brewery. Then it's like we're back in high school. Besties, as if he hasn't spent the last year acting like we didn't used to talk on the phone every day. It's infuriating."

"Oh, no, Hanna," Faith said, fuming as she glared at Rhys. "I've always liked him. Everyone does. And Clay, he loves him, too. Says he's the best damned assistant brewer he could ask for. But no one treats my friend like a dirty little secret, no one. What the hell is that? You can't let him get away with that crap, Hanna. Tell him to stick it where the sun doesn't shine next time."

She laughed. "You've been hanging out with too many children lately. 'Stick it where the sun doesn't shine?' Whatever happened to shove it up your—"

"Hey, did someone order booze and cake?" Hunter said loudly, gesturing to Zoey, who was holding two cake plates.

"Yay! I love you," Faith said, kissing him on the cheek as she took her champagne glass. "You, too, little Z." She pulled the little girl onto her lap and hugged her tight.

Hanna ate cake and drank more champagne while she pretended to ignore Rhys and Lena, who had moved off to the side of the other dancers and were continuing to argue. Then finally, she heard Lena say, "So that's it then. It's over?"

Rhys mumbled something and stared at his feet.

Lena let out an irritated huff and stalked off, leaving him there looking like a fool. Hanna's first instinct was to get up and go to him, make sure he was okay. But as she watched him watch Lena walk away, it was the same look he'd had on his face when he'd told her they were better as friends, and she got mad all over again.

What was with him and commitment? He'd certainly dated

over the years, but never anyone serious. Hanna had secretly hoped it was because deep down he knew they were supposed to be together. But then he'd burst that bubble and spent the next year single... until Lena. Now he was repeating the same cycle. She didn't understand.

"I want to dance," Faith said. "Zoey, are you ready to shake your groove thang?"

The little girl grinned. "Yes, but you can't dance. You have a broken foot."

"You just watch me." Faith popped up on her good foot, grabbed one of her crutches, and hopped out onto the dance floor. "Get your butts out here." She waved to Hunter, Zoey, and Hanna. "Don't leave me hangin'."

Hunter and Zoey hurried to join her, but Hanna shook her head, politely declining. She wasn't really in the mood to dance, and thankfully Faith let it go.

Hanna was just about to go grab another drink when Drew hopped up on the small, temporary stage where the DJ was set up in the corner. "Hello everyone. Thanks for joining us tonight for our Christmas Eve celebration. Noel and I are very thankful you could be here."

The crowd clapped and yelled out congratulations.

"Thank you, thank you. You're in for a treat, because the boys and I were supposed to make good on a bet last week at the holiday carnival, but due to some unforeseen family circumstances, it didn't happen. So tonight we have a gift for Noel, her sisters, and all of you. Noel?" He waved for her to join them as Clay set a chair in the middle of the stage.

Noel, shaking her head and blushing furiously, climbed up on the stage. She was wearing a gorgeous white mermaid dress with a red sash and matching red stilettos.

"Have a seat, babe." Drew grinned.

"What are you doing?" Noel asked with a laugh, but Hanna

was certain she already knew. They hadn't yet made good on their bet to sing "Santa Baby," and Drew was making it happen in front of all their guests.

"Making good on a bet." He winked, ran off the stage, and disappeared behind a partition screen that seemed to have appeared out of nowhere. A few moments later, the music started and Clay, Brian, Drew, and Rhys ran out from behind the screen. Hanna was surprised to see the big grin on Rhys's face, considering he'd just had a blow up with Lena. But that was Rhys, always the one who could compartmentalize. She was equally surprised to see Brian on stage with the rest of them since he hadn't been in the losing cart when the bet was made. But he was such a fun-loving guy that it probably wasn't hard for the others to convince him to play along.

Each of them were wearing short, red-sequined dresses that were cinched at the waist with forest green belts and had white faux fur lining the top of the bodice and the bottom of the skirt. They'd completed the look with green knee-high suede boots.

The wedding guests all cheered, while Noel clapped her hand over her mouth and shook her head in disbelief.

The men started lip-syncing and swaying to the music, doing their best white-man's-overbite moves. Then they paired up and tried to do some complicated hand-to-foot moves that didn't even match the music. Brian tripped over his own feet and pitched head-first straight into Clay, causing them both to go down in a heap.

The roar of laughter from the crowd was deafening, but Rhys and Drew ignored their partners in crime, moving on to twirling each other around as if nothing had happened. Unable to keep from cracking up, Brian and Clay got to their feet just in time for the grand finale.

As the song came to an end, all four men started

shimmying their hips, and the next thing Hanna knew, Clay, Brian, and Rhys grabbed at the fabric at their hips and ripped their dresses right off. They spun around, bending over so the guests could see the writing on their fur-lined boxers.

Congrats, Drew & Noel!

Only Noel never saw it, because just as the guys were getting ready to strip, Drew covered her eyes with his hands and made a shocked *O* face for the crowd.

The guests loved it and went wild with their applause, hooting and hollering, while Hanna just sat there staring at Rhys as he gathered his outfit and hurried back to the safety of the privacy screen. He was gorgeous and more muscular than she'd imagined he would be, and even in his fur-lined boxers, she found him the sexiest man she'd ever seen.

Once all of the guys disappeared to get redressed, Hanna made her way into the house, used the facilities, touched up her makeup, and then reemerged feeling like a new woman.

She stopped in the kitchen to grab a glass of water. After downing half of it, she turned around and ran smack into Rhys's chest. His hands came up to steady her, and her skin tingled all over from his touch.

"Whoa. Careful," he said, smiling down at her. He was back in his suit, but he hadn't bothered to redo his tie. "What's the hurry?"

"No hurry. Try not to sneak up on people, huh?" She tried to sidestep him, suddenly irritated again about how he'd broken up with Lena right before the performance. It had been a repeat of how things had gone down with them a year ago. The realization that she was mad that he'd broken up with Lena almost made her laugh. Two hours ago, she'd have been ecstatic about the news. Now she was just annoyed.

"Wait, Hanna. Where are you going? I thought we could talk."

She stared up into his earnest expression and shook her head. "I don't think so, Rhys. If you need to talk to someone, try one of your buddies."

He frowned, his brows drawing together in confusion. "But *you're* one of my buddies."

"Is that what you think? That we're friends? That we can just call each other up and chit-chat, make plans, and listen to each other's problems?" she asked.

"Sure. We could do that. We used to do that all the time."

"Right. Then we didn't. I think that means we're not the friends we used to be." She patted him on the arm. "Maybe Clay has time to chat. I'm going back to the party."

"Hanna!" He strode forward and jumped in front of her to block her from leaving the kitchen. "It's you I want to talk to. Lena and I—"

She held her hand up, stopping him. "I don't want to talk about Lena. Haven't you figured it out yet, Rhys? We're not friends anymore. We haven't been since you dumped me at Abby's wedding."

"Hey," he said, sounding angry. "I didn't dump you. I just said I thought it was better if we didn't date for the sake of our friendship. You agreed."

"Did I? Did I really? Is that how you remember it?" She knew she'd agreed, because what else was she going to say? But it hadn't been her idea, and it certainly hadn't been her idea for him to back all the way off and ghost on her.

"Yeah, that's how I remember it." He moved in closer, making her body ache for him even though she was thoroughly pissed off now. "And then I don't know what happened, but I know I miss the hell out of you. Can't we just go back to the way we were before? Best friends who can talk about anything?"

"Best friends?"

"Yes."

"Who can talk about anything you say?" She eyed him suspiciously.

His confidence seemed to falter a little as he said, "Sure. I know I could use someone to talk to right now."

"Right now." She pursed her lips and nodded. It was clear he wanted to talk about his breakup with Lena, but she wasn't having it. The last time they'd had a real conversation was right before he'd started dating Lena. She was no one's second choice. And she was about to prove it.

"All right. Let's talk about this." She grabbed his shirt, yanked him to her, and kissed him with everything she had. He stiffened slightly but then opened his mouth, inviting her passion and wrapping his arms around her. With a small gasp, he tilted his head and deepened the kiss, making her toes curl with pleasure.

When she pulled back, breathless and wanting, she gazed up at him and asked in a sultry voice, "Is that what *buddies* do, Rhys?"

"Uh, um, buddies?" he asked, his eyes glazed with lust.

She patted his chest and said, "You think about it and let me know what you come up with." Then she turned on her heel and sailed out of the kitchen and back to the party.

DEANNA'S BOOK LIST

Pyper Rayne Novels:
Spirits, Stilettos, and a Silver Bustier
Spirits, Rock Stars, and a Midnight Chocolate Bar
Spirits, Beignets, and a Bayou Biker Gang
Spirits, Diamonds, and a Drive-thru Daiquiri Stand

Jade Calhoun Novels:
Haunted on Bourbon Street
Witches of Bourbon Street
Demons of Bourbon Street
Angels of Bourbon Street
Shadows of Bourbon Street
Incubus of Bourbon Street
Bewitched on Bourbon Street
Hexed on Bourbon Street

Witches of Keating Hollow:
Soul of the Witch
Heart of the Witch

Spirit of the Witch
Dreams of the Witch
Courage of the Witch

Last Witch Standing:
Soulless at Sunset
Bloodlust By Midnight
Bitten At Daybreak

Witch Island Brides:
The Vampire's Last Dance
The Wolf's New Year Bride
The Warlock's Enchanted Kiss
The Shifter's First Bite

Crescent City Fae Novels:
Influential Magic
Irresistible Magic
Intoxicating Magic

Destiny Novels:
Defining Destiny
Accepting Fate

ABOUT THE AUTHOR

New York Times and USA Today bestselling author, Deanna Chase, is a native Californian, transplanted to the slower paced lifestyle of southeastern Louisiana. When she isn't writing, she is often goofing off with her husband in New Orleans or playing with her two shih tzu dogs. For more information and updates on newest releases visit her website at deannachase.com.

62564204R00145

Made in the USA
Columbia, SC
03 July 2019